John McLaughlin

RED SKY AT MORNING

A NOVEL

Library of Congress Control Number: 2009912262

Published by John McLaughlin Books
Peoria, Arizona
www.johnmclaughlinbooks.com

© 2009 John McLaughlin. All rights reserved.
Published by John McLaughlin Books 2010
Printed by Lightning Source Inc. (US)
Cover and interior art work by Jonathan McLaughlin (jonmclaughlin.com)

Printed in the United States of America
978-0-615-33493-6

"Out of every one hundred men, ten shouldn't even be there. Eighty are just targets. Nine are the real fighters, and we are lucky to have them for they make the battle. Ah, but the one … one is a warrior, and he will bring the others back."

—HERICLETUS, circa 500 BC

Dedicated to
Arizona BLM Law Enforcement Rangers

For my mother
Who always stressed the importance of reading
And following your dreams

AUTHOR'S NOTE

his story is the sequel to *Our Time in the Sun*, and as such, it is a historically accurate account of an Old West group of lawmen, the Arizona Rangers. This action-filled novel completes the epic story of the Rangers in the Arizona Territory of 1901-09, culminating in their political demise.

For those of you with a special historical interest in the Arizona Rangers, most of the major gun battles in this story are actual incidents the old Rangers participated in along the border in a time long, long ago. The historical incidents and associated violence that was present over one hundred years ago along the border with Mexico is not unlike many of today's accounts.

John D. McLaughlin

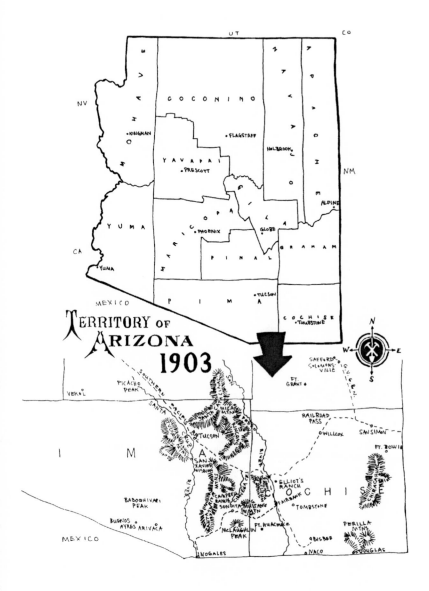

TERRITORY of ARIZONA 1903

RED SKY AT MORNING

ɕ

CHAPTER ONE
Arizona Territory 1906

The saguaro cactus stood tall; reaching out with its giant arms, extending high toward the heavens as the sun rose delicately in the morning sky behind the huge sentinel. Marveling at the scene before him, Joaquin Campbell reined in his impatient paint horse. "Easy now, boy. I reckon we got time to take a look at this big feller."

He quickly threw a slip knot with the pack rope around the saddle horn and tipped his Stetson hat back to display a white forehead above his tanned boyish-looking face. The paint horse stood still as commanded, but stamped his front hoof repeatedly, showing his displeasure at not continuing on up the trail into the Rincon Mountains. Joaquin's gaze took in the giant cactus with its numerous arms—the golden red sky afire beyond it against the horizon of white clouds. *Gosh, it's got at least ...thirty arms ...maybe more?* It was late spring in the Arizona desert. The saguaro would soon be displaying its beautiful white flowers; they would then give way to the red "tunas" or fruit as autumn progressed. His old friend Elliott had told him long ago the fruit contained many seeds, but only a select few ever germinated to become these giant sentinels dotting the Sonoran desert landscape.

The paint horse whirled around abruptly, interrupting Joaquin's thoughts. The secured pack rope almost encircled him, the pack horse now startled as well. His dog, Solo Vino, trotted up the trail behind them, panting in the heat of the day. Joaquin reined his horse around, removed the slip knot in the pack rope, and lightly touched his spurs, letting the cow pony know it was time to progress up into the mountains. *Best quit lollygaggin' and pay attention to business.* The dog quietly skirted around them and disappeared around a switchback in the trail above them.

Joaquin Campbell was twenty years old, closer to twenty-one. He straightened himself in the saddle. The silver badge on his shirt front briefly reflected the bright sunlight into a piliated woodpecker's eyes as he pecked away while perched atop one of the saguaro cactus' arms. Campbell had enlisted in the Arizona Rangers two years prior, and he had done some serious growing up during that time. He was forced to kill outlaws and bandits, fight another Ranger who had tarnished his badge in the line of duty, and along the way he had become one of the better lawmen in the Ranger company despite his young age and inexperience.

His assignment was simple—find and arrest a certain rustler living in the Rincon Mountains. If he found stolen livestock, he was to trail them back with him along with the arrestee. No small task; hence he brought his old companion, Solo Vino, who he knew could handle the livestock while he concentrated on his prisoner. He and his dog had trailed cattle together for years at home at his folks' ranch on Cienega Creek north of the small village of Sonoita in southeastern Arizona Territory.

As he rode along, his pack mule in tow and his dog in the lead, Joaquin thought about what he needed to do and most importantly how to do it safely. Before he realized it, he had departed the lower desert country with its saguaro-palo verde landscape and entered the more open grasslands transition zone. Catclaw, mesquite, and grama grasses resided in the rocky countryside. As he ascended farther into the rugged country, the mesquite and oak disappeared with Mexican and piñon pines becoming dominant species, and he was thankful to ride in the shade of the larger trees.

It took him almost four hours to reach a point on the mountain he felt was close to the rustler's cabin site. His friend Elliott had advised him of crossing a small drainage where he could water the horse and mule. From there he was to continue up the trail another half-mile or so beyond a large rock outcropping to a flat area replete with open Ponderosa pine woodlands and green ferns.

He had no trouble finding either location. Joaquin dismounted in the flat open area high in the Rincon Mountains, and tied his saddle horse and pack mule securely to smaller trees. Loosening the cinch on his saddle horse, he knelt down and gently patted his dog's head, then scratched behind Solo Vino's wooly ears. The old dog's eye lids closed, his tongue protruding from a mouth that smiled up at him. "*Oye*, Solo. You're the best friend a man could ever have!"

Joaquin withdrew jerky and biscuits from his saddle bags. *That Elliott ... he's some older now, but he sure remembers this country.* As Joaquin sat leaning against a large Ponderosa pine tree, he observed the area was exactly as Elliott had described to him. He was not very hungry, but he knew he should eat something and would need his strength soon enough. So he washed the jerky and most of a biscuit down with cool water from his canteen. Sighing, he stood and stretched his slender frame, walked to his horse, and pulled the .30-.40 1895 Winchester rifle from the saddle scabbard. He looked at the dog and smiled. "Come on boy. Let's see if we can find this rustler."

After a mile or so of walking, the terrain flattened out even more. As it was open pine woodland, Joaquin could see well ahead as he strode silently in the thick, soft pine needles layering the forest floor. He hissed at the dog; squinting, he peered ahead knowing that others could see as well as he could. The dog quietly dropped back behind him as instructed.

Smoke in the air? The young Ranger sensed he was close to the cabin and slowed his approach accordingly. Then he saw the small cabin in the distance tucked back in the trees. *Somebody's home.* Joaquin stepped behind a large Ponderosa pine tree, peering closely at the cabin and surroundings. Solo Vino dropped to the ground at his feet. The clear mountain air smelled good to him, the dominant smell of the dry pine needles overriding the smoke from the cabin. No one—nothing moved.

The rustler's name was Harvey Manfield and supposedly lived alone. But Joaquin knew better than to take that information for granted. He looked at the barn and corrals located some fifty yards from the cabin. There were two horses, a couple of mules and ten head of cattle in the corrals. Joaquin looked closer and noted the stolen brands on several of the cows. One of the horses, a bald-faced sorrel, was in a corral by itself. *Maybe a visitor?* He decided to work on the premise there were at least two men in the cabin. He stood silently ... waiting ... watching. He recalled Elliott's warning, *Patience boy! Them thet gets in a hurry is likely to get their fool heads blowed off.* Solo Vino remained quiet at his feet; the dog appeared as though he was asleep, then one eye lid opened as the young Ranger levered a cartridge into the chamber of his rifle, carefully releasing the hammer.

A good half-hour passed—still no movement outside the cabin. Smoke drifted out of the chimney, the column swirled up toward the sky, bending occasionally in the gentle morning breeze. The cabin door opened abruptly and a man stepped out onto the porch. Hatless, he stood with a tin cup in his hand. Joaquin's heartbeat quickened. *Manfield!* Joaquin recognized the description: the beard, bald head with minimal matted hair along the sides, the big barrel chest, and protruding belly.

Manfield finished drinking from the cup, set it down on the porch and headed toward Joaquin, stopping at the outhouse some fifty yards from the cabin. He dropped his suspenders as he entered the outhouse. The man didn't appear to be armed. What was Elliott's favorite saying? *Even a blind hog gits an acorn now an' agin.* Joaquin's grim face broke into a smile for just an instant.

His rifle at the ready, Joaquin cocked the hammer on his rifle then inched slowly toward the outhouse, keeping to the cover of trees while watching for any movement from the cabin. He took final cover behind another large Ponderosa tree near the outhouse.

Moments passed. Joaquin thought of Elliott again, his old friend and mentor. The old gunman and Ranger had resigned from the Arizona Rangers more then a year ago. *I sure miss that old man.* Elliott had married his sister Megan Campbell and ... *hold it!* Joaquin heard shuffling inside the outhouse. The door opened with a loud creak. Manfield stepped out, slipping the suspenders back over his shoulders. Joaquin raised the rifle to his shoulder, swallowing hard. His heartbeat quickened as he stepped out from behind the tree. "Don't move, Manfield. Arizona Rangers! You're under arrest."

The rustler's hands reached for his pants pocket as he turned toward the young Ranger. Elliott's voice rang in Joaquin's ears: *Always watch their hands, mi'jo. It's them hands thet will kill ya, son.*

"Get your hands in the air. *Now!*"

Eyes wide, his mouth open, Manfield slowly raised both hands in the air as he looked into the muzzle of the

Winchester rifle. He started to speak.

"Shut up!" Joaquin hissed. "Get down on your knees." As the rustler reluctantly complied, Joaquin slowly moved to a position behind him. He took a quick look over his shoulder at the cabin, and seeing no immediate danger, spoke curtly, "Cross your legs at the ankles." Again the man hesitated, but complied as Joaquin jabbed the rifle barrel roughly into his back.

Joaquin reached into his jacket pocket and withdrew the heavy metal handcuffs and stepped down hard on top of the man's crossed feet. "Place your hands behind your back, Manfield."

Joaquin released the hammer on his rifle and laid it on the pine needle-laden forest floor behind him. Quickly, he secured the man's huge left wrist, then with difficulty, the right wrist in the handcuffs. Joaquin perspired and breathed heavily in the cool morning air. *It shouldn't be so hot up here. It's 8,000 feet for cryin' out loud.*

As he turned to retrieve his weapon, the loud report of a rifle reverberated into the quiet forest. Something tugged hard at his Stetson hat, jerking it off his head. Joaquin grabbed for his rifle, cocked the hammer, and dove to the ground, rolling several times. More gunshots. Bullets thudded into the ground where he had been just seconds before. He rolled to a stop behind a large pine tree, looking through the fixed sights of his rifle. Breathing hard, he saw another man charging him from the cabin. Bark flew from the tree that provided him some cover from his assailant. Debris flew into his eyes, momentarily blinding him.

From his left Manfield screamed, "Kill the son-of-a-bitch, dammit! *Finish him!*"

"I got him, by Gawd," the man rasped as he ran toward the downed Ranger, levering another round in his rifle. He stopped in mid-stride, raising the rifle.

Joaquin's vision cleared. The rustler was wide-eyed with tobacco juice running down his unkempt, sweating face. Joaquin shot first, his .30-.40 rounds tearing through the man's torso once, then twice with the rustler knocked back and to the ground.

Joaquin was up and running toward the downed outlaw. The man's hand moved toward his rifle. Joaquin shot him twice more. *Don't ever give them bad men a leg up, boy. You do an' they'll kill ya ... or worse.* As he looked quickly at the cabin and the surrounding area, he heard scuffling in the brush. Manfield ran awkwardly off into the woods, his handcuffed arms flopping behind him. Joaquin pointed at the fleeing felon and yelled, "Take him, Sol." The quiet dog leaped into action.

Breathing hard, Joaquin reached the outlaw he had just shot. He reached down, picked up the man's rifle, and ejected the remaining shells from the magazine tube. Tossing the firearm some distance away, he squatted near the man surveying the scene. No movement came from the cabin. The man's eyes were open. Blood mixed with tobacco juice trickled from his open mouth, pooling beneath him on the forest floor.

Wasting no more time, Joaquin ran, zigzagging toward the front door of the cabin. He reached it safely without taking fire. Leaning hard against the log walls, he tried to catch his breath as well as his thoughts. He laid down his rifle, drew the .45 Colt revolver from his pistol belt, then took three quick breaths, holding each one a few seconds. It helped calm him some. Elliott's advice rang in his ears again, *Move quick when goin' in an' don't never stand in the doorway—they'll be waitin' an' kill ya fer shore.* Turning, he dove in low through the entrance to the cabin, rolling on his right side, slamming hard against chairs and a wooden table in the center of the floor. With his six-shooter out in front of him, his weak hand supporting his strong hand, he quickly cleared the one-room cabin finding no one. Slowly releasing the air from his lungs, he sighed deeply.

Retrieving his rifle outside, Joaquin carefully cleared the small barn and other small out buildings. *Two men ... what I'd figgered. God almighty, I damned near got my head blowed off. What would Carmie say?* He decided he wouldn't tell his wife. Why worry her? Besides she had recently suffered a miscarriage and was six months pregnant with a second child. His thoughts were interrupted by a man screaming at the top of his lungs down the ridge from the cabin. Joaquin's dog barked excitedly.

He found Manfield a ways down from the ridge-top. Solo Vino was astride the rustler, his teeth bared, growling in the man's face.

"Git this dammed dog off me!" The man writhed back and forth.

Joaquin took his time. He hissed at the dog, who withdrew reluctantly behind him.

The rustler sat upright. After regaining his composure and seeing the lawman's young face, he ordered, "You best keep that—"

Joaquin reached down, roughly grasped his shirt front, and hit him hard in the face. "I reckon it's time we got something straight." He jerked the man back to a sitting position. "You run again, you even try to talk to me without my permission, I'll kill you." Joaquin's eyes narrowed, jaws clenched. "You *understand* me, you filthy *son-of-a-bitch?*"

The rustler swallowed hard, blood dripped from his mouth; sweat ran in rivulets down his dirty face and neck. He swallowed again, fear showing in his wild eyes as he nodded his bald head, careful not to speak.

CHAPTER TWO
Naco, Arizona Territory

The small border town of Naco in the Arizona Territory was raucous to say the least, but its sister city across the border in Mexico was far worse. Ranger Bill Calhoun laughed out loud as he thought about the recent memo from Captain Tom Rynning, head of the Arizona Rangers.

Rynning had mandated all his Rangers to steer clear of the Mexican side of the border in Naco—personal or professional business. A recent international incident had occurred there involving *gringos*, who were running guns across the border and selling them to the rebelling Yaquis. Several Mexican Rurales had been killed and tension existed between the two countries.

Calhoun walked easily on the plank side-walk, his spurs clinking musically. He strode past several saloons and brothels. Pausing in the shadows of an alley, he rolled his cigarette leisurely, lit it then drew deeply inhaling the smoke. The cigarette glowed in the darkness, illuminating a dark face under a large flat-brimmed hat with a pointed crown.

The Ranger wore a long-sleeved cotton shirt with a buttoned-up vest covering his torso. On the left side of the vest, a five-pointed silver star glimmered briefly in the dimly lit street. His cotton pants were tucked inside his high-topped riding boots. As Calhoun continued down the dusty street, the leather pistol belt and holster creaked with the weight of fully-loaded cartridge loops and the encased .45 Colt revolver that hung on the right side near his waist.

As he thought of his current mission in Naco, his face turned grim. He knew he was dealing with a rough bunch—thugs, thieves, murderers—all of them making money from running guns. A helluva lot of money was generated running guns over the border into Mexico to sell to the Yaqui Indians, and anyone else. It didn't matter much who got the guns as long as they paid big money for them. Calhoun took another drag on his cigarette.

Captain Rynning had sent him down to Naco to find those responsible for the gun running operation. The Mexican government was very upset with American firearms finding their way to the Yaquis, who were openly rebelling against Mexico. The situation was getting out of control with the line riders on both sides of the border unable to cope with the crisis. Naco appeared to be the focal point of the gun running operation. Calhoun watched silently as two drunken men staggered past him attempting to hold each other upright.

The small town of 500 residents was located on the major route from Bisbee, Arizona to Cananea, Mexico, the location of a large mining operation run by W.C. Greene. Due to the proximity of the shipping route and the Mexican border, Naco naturally had become the scene for massive smuggling activities. Local officials were believed to be in "cahoots" with outlaws and bandits from both sides of the border.

The Ranger crossed the street, tossing the remnants of his cigarette to the ground. Calhoun's orders were clear. Find those responsible and report back to Captain Rynning. The Rangers would then mount an operation to arrest all those responsible. He had only been in town for three days and already had several leads in the case. He was meeting with an informant this evening.

Calhoun stopped, removed his Ranger badge from his vest and tucked it into his pants pocket. Stepping up on the board sidewalk, he entered the loud *cantina*. He worked his way through the smoke-laden room full of drunken customers packed in like sardines in a can. Calhoun stopped at a wooden stairway near the back of the large room. The stairs led up to a series of rooms located along a balcony that overlooked the saloon itself. A man with a small derby hat perched on his large head stepped in front of him, placing a hand on the Ranger's chest. He growled, "You want to go upstairs with the whores, you pay up first, sonny."

Calhoun looked steadily at the heavy-set, stocky pimp with ugly scars on his face. He took in the deadly blackjack tucked in the man's belt. Smiling at the thug, he said, "Why, sure thing. How much for Juanita?"

"She's busy. Pick another." Beads of sweat ran down the swarthy face.

"Well, I ... uh ... can't do that. She's *extra* special. If ya know what I mean." Calhoun grinned as he reached into his pocket, withdrawing $10.00. He handed the money to the thug. "Five dollars for Juanita, five dollars extra just for you, my friend ... *if* I get her now."

The thug thought about it, rubbing his face. Abruptly, he pocketed the money. "Wait here." He ascended the stairs and walked to the third room down the hallway. Without knocking, he opened the door and stepped inside, closing the door behind him. Moments later, he reappeared, towing an unconscious man behind him by the shirt collar. The thug dragged the man down the hallway to the steps then shoved him down the stairs. Calhoun stepped aside as the unfortunate man bounced past him to the dirty saloon floor.

"You got one hour with her, cowboy," the thug

snarled, "after that you'll get what he got if ya ain't gone."

Calhoun bounded up the steps past the thug, made his way to the open door, and slipped into the small darkened room. A dimly-lit kerosene lamp was perched on a table to the left of a dirty cot. A young Mexican woman sat naked on the edge of the cot. She took a long drink from the whiskey bottle in her left hand. She peered at the Ranger in front of her, wiping her mouth with the back of her other hand.

"Yew again, *guero*?"

"Yep."

"*¿Tiene el dinero?* Ya got mah money?"

"*Lo tengo.* I got it." The Ranger moved to where he was standing in front of the woman. "I reckon it's enough to get you outta this hell hole, Juanita." He placed his thumbs in his gun belt. "But you'll get nothing till you give me the name of who's runnin' the guns—*el jefe*—the head honcho, not the soldiers."

Juanita took another long pull at the bottle, mulling over the offer. "*Me van a matar. Eef* they find out, they *weel* keel me, *chota*." She rested the bottle on her knee, her bloated frightened face looking into Bill Calhoun's eyes.

"Give me the information, Juanita. '*Horita*. I reckon I don't have time to play games."

She beckoned for him to move closer to her. As he leaned forward, she whispered in his ear.

"*Who?*" His dark frowning face almost touched hers. She whispered a little louder. "*What?*"

The door to the room flew open. Two men burst in, both holding revolvers. Calhoun instinctively reached for his six-shooter as a gun exploded. He grimaced as he felt the bullet tear through his abdomen. Drawing his revolver, he pulled back on the trigger, fanning the hammer. His handgun spouted flame and lead. One of the assailants was flung back against the wall. He slid down the wall, smearing it with his blood.

Juanita screamed. Another gun spoke. Calhoun felt the rounds slicing through his chest, then his neck. He summoned all of his remaining strength as he staggered backwards, fanning the hammer of his revolver again and again.

***

Calhoun lay dying, his blood pooling underneath him on the dirty wooden floor. He heard footsteps. Men talking in whispered excited voices. "What about that sneakin' Ranger? All hell's gonna break loose now on account of this *whore* gittin' too smart for her britches." The Ranger heard several individuals scuffling in the room. A woman gasped.

"You're gonna pay for your loose mouth!"

"*Por favor, Señores*, I deedn't say any theeng," the woman pleaded, "*Don't—*" A high-pitched scream echoed in the room, replaced by a sickening gurgling sound.

"You *lying* whore," her assailant rasped. Another muffled scream

Calhoun struggled to use his hand. Ever so slowly, he mustered his remaining strength and dabbed his fingers in the congealing blood surrounding him on the dingy floor. Reaching out, he lifted the small rug under the table. *Got to ....*

Moments passed. Calhoun realized he could no longer move either his arms or legs. Pain stabbed at his chest, neck, and abdomen. *So this is what it's like to die.* He closed his eyes, grimacing as he sighed loudly. Hearing a revolver cocking, he opened his weary eyes and stared into the muzzle of a .45 Colt. His eyes flicked quickly to the man and his arm holding the gun close to his face. *You! Juanita didn't lie.*

The deafening roar of the explosion filled the dim, blood splattered room at the top of the stairs.

CHAPTER THREE

Elliott led the *grulla* saddle horse behind him as he sauntered along the San Pedro River bottom south of his ranch house. *Gawd, but I do love the spring!* He paused briefly, peering up into the canopy of the numerous cottonwood trees; the bright green leaves bending ever so slightly in the afternoon breeze, momentarily displaying the bright blue southwestern sky above. The gray bay with the black mane and tail softly nudged his back.

A boy's voice broke the silence, "Have we got there yet, Dad?"

A broad smile appeared across Elliott's tanned, leathery face. "I reckon we're about there, *mijo*," referring affectionately in Spanish to his son. He turned, facing the young boy astride his horse. Reaching out, he stroked the smooth neck of his horse. "Ol' Viento, why, he's jest as restless as you, Timmy boy." He re-adjusted the boy's wooden crutches hanging from the saddle horn.

Elliott thought of his life—as a young cowpuncher trailing cattle herds from Texas to Kansas, and later to California; fighting the fierce Apache, his gun fighting days, and lately his years as an Arizona Ranger and rancher. *It's been a hard life, but a good 'un in a lot o' ways.* Relieved to be finished with all the killing, he was content to enjoy the rest of his life here on the ranch with those he loved. It had been a long time coming. He was fifty-six years old, and some days he felt it; other days, why, he felt like plumb lettin' the badger out. Chuckling at the thought, he broke into a sly grin.

Savoring the quiet, the old Ranger led the horse down the trail for another half-mile, stopping in a flat, clear portion of the green riparian area. He dropped the reins, and the dun horse stood still. Elliott removed the wooden crutches from the saddle then gently lifted the young boy, setting him down next to the horse. Hanging on to the stirrup, Timmy Campbell secured the crutches under his arms, and looked up at Elliott, "You'll let me shoot your gun, won't you?"

"Thet's the idée, boy. You been houndin' me fer weeks." He retrieved the old pistol belt and holster from the saddle horn. Encased in the weathered, leather holster greased down with skunk grease was a well-used .45 Colt revolver, its worn brown butt still displaying the inscription, "*M y J.*" He slung the pistol belt over his shoulder. "Come on, *mijo*. Let's walk o'er to thet big cottonwood tree."

The young boy moved slowly but steadily behind Elliott, one foot turned in from the polio. Walking was difficult, but he was determined to do it on his own. Elliott sat in the grass; Timmy dropped his crutches and sat down heavily next to him.

Elliott set the pistol belt down and began to build himself a cigarette. He peered at the twelve-year old boy next to him as he licked the cigarette paper, stuck the cigarette in the corner of his mouth, and lit it. Smoke drifted lazily from his nostrils, then his mouth. "I reckon we'll do some shore 'nough shootin' today, but you an' me ... we got some talkin' to do first."

He took another drag on the cigarette. "A gun is a tool, boy. Jest like an axe or a shovel, 'ceptin' it kin kill you quicker an' from a lot farther away." His face hardened as he spoke, "Treat ever' gun like it's loaded an' understand thet it kin hurt or plumb kill you or somebody else. Ain't no play thing. You gittin' my drift, boy?"

"Yes, sir."

"You shore?"

"Yes, sir!"

The old Ranger smiled, reached down and picked up the pistol belt, drawing the heavy Colt revolver from the weathered holster. He palmed it, keeping the barrel pointed away from himself and the boy. "Never point a gun at someone less'n you're figgerin' on killin' 'em." His eyes narrowed. "If the need's there to kill, then do it, *quick-like,* don't *never* hesitate."

"I don't want to harm anybody. I just want to learn to shoot," the boy returned softly.

"*Good boy.* I shore hope you never have to kill—" Elliott hesitated. "But you ever do, you recollect what I told ya, you hear?"

The boy thought a moment, pursed his lips, "I'll remember."

"All right. Let's git to it," said Elliott. He showed the boy how to load and unload the revolver, to always cock the single-action six-shooter, aim while holding the heavy handgun with both hands, and to shoot quick and straight. The boy was eager to learn. He practiced hard at becoming a better shot. Then he insisted on more practice, asking questions, furthering his insight on how the gun functioned and how to become a better shooter.

The orange sun was almost set in the western sky when they finished shooting. It suddenly appeared almost blood red. Elliott smiled and pointed. "Red sky at the morning—sailor's warning; red sky at night—sailor's delight."

"Sir?"

"Aw, nothin',Timmy. I jest took me a gander at thet purty sunset, an' thought 'bout what an ol' scout I used to work fer in the Army once told me."

Interested, the boy looked up at the old Ranger.

"Who was he?"

Grunting, Elliott replied, "Grijalva. Don't reckon his name matters as much as what he meant though." He placed both his hands on the boy's shoulders. "Tomorrow's bound to be a good weather day what with the sky red at night. Now, if there's ever a red sky at mornin', why, *cuidado*—watch out! It'll plumb be a badun' fer shore."

"Where did that saying come from, Elliott?"

Elliott rubbed the back of his neck then his jaw. "Well now, I don't rightly know, son. I'd say from them sailors way out yonder at sea."

"Do you believe it to be true?" asked Timmy.

"Yessir. I reckon so. A red sky at morning has meant nothin' but trouble fer me o'er the years." He nodded his head as he looked again at the ebbing sunset.

Elliott showed the boy how to clean the old revolver. "Always keep 'er clean, *mijo*. If you don't, she'll fail ya." He sighed. "Then you'll have nobody to blame but yourself."

"Yes sir." Timmy wiped the outside of the cylinder with a lightly oiled rag. "The engraving on the butt plate? The '*M y J*? They're for your wife and son, aren't they, sir?"

The old Ranger bit his lower lip, took a deep breath and exhaled. "Thet's right, *mijo*. Maria and Joaquin. Well, the first Joaquin thet is. Your uncle was named Joaquin, too, later on."

The boy set the gun down in his lap. "You loved them a lot, didn't you, Elliott?"

"I reckon I still do. Time won't never change thet none." He paused, his eyes brightened. "Them Injuns took 'em from me years ago when I was jest a young feller, Timmy. But they're still with me. Ever' day I kin see 'em, right here beside me, close-like." He patted the ground beside him.

"I'm so sorry," the boy whispered, feeling the older man's agony in re-visiting the past.

"No need to be. I know they're both in a better place now." Elliott reached over and hugged the boy. "I've got me a good life now—with you an' your Mama."

Timmy smiled, "I'm glad you're my Dad, Elliott, and married to my Mom."

A soft voice spoke suddenly behind them, "You two finished? It'll be dark soon." The boy and old Ranger turned quickly. Megan Campbell stood with both hands on her hips. Her brown hair was done up in a bun in the back. A smattering of gray showed near her temples. She wore a red and white checkered apron over the top of a long blue cotton dress. Elliott gazed longingly at the woman he loved and thought, *she's the best lookin' gal plumb west o' the Mississippi River, hoss.*

Elliott stood, smiling. "Wel-l-l, if it ain't thet lil' school marm I heerd tell of—"

"Don't you school marm me, Samuel T. Elliott."

"Yes ma'am. We'll come along *real* quiet-like." Elliott laughed, holding up his hands in surrender. "Jest don't be pullin' us along by the ear." He walked over to her, giving her a big hug and a kiss. "Thet'd look plumb awful in front o' the neighbors."

It was Megan's turn to laugh. "Come along you two. Let's go back to the house. Hao Li's waiting for us—supper's on the table."

Megan had been teaching before Elliott married her about a year ago. He had taken to her son as if the boy were his own. She and Tim had moved in with Elliott on his ranch along the San Pedro River. Shortly thereafter, he had resigned from the Arizona Rangers and begun ranching full-time, slowly building his small herd. His old Chinese friend Hao-Li had remained at the ranch helping take care of things and tending to his large garden next to the house.

I got me a life worth livin' agin with Meg and Timmy. But there was a time, I reckon. He felt for the old brown rosary in his pocket and reflected on his long-standing promise to pray the rosary daily in the hope God would forgive him for his violent past and allow him to join his first wife and son in heaven one day. He would never forget them or his promise. *Gawd, I'm awful sorry fer all the killin' I've done. They was real bad 'uns thet I done in, but—.*

Now he had been given the opportunity to live a life worth living once again—a fine wife and son to care for, look after. As he and Megan walked together under the canopy of the large cottonwood trees, their arms around each other, he thought, *as old as I am, I hope it ain't too late fer me.* Viento followed along with Timmy in the saddle, the tapadero stirrups swinging back and forth beneath the horse's belly. The sun had dipped below the horizon. The moonless sky transformed into an inky darkness as the trio made it back to the barn.

CHAPTER FOUR
Naco, Arizona Territory

It was early morning. Dawn ushered in the morning with orange and red illuminating the Arizona sky. Joaquin Campbell stepped down from the board sidewalk in front of Hotel Naco, a two-story adobe building along Naco's D Street, the main north-south thoroughfare. He took in a deep breath of spring air, surveying the small town from where he stood in the quiet, dusty street. A freight car loaded with copper rumbled north through a large opening in the border fence along the railroad tracks, startling him momentarily.

Joaquin started down the street, his spurs clinking dully in the sandy soil. His father's old pistol belt was strapped around his waist, the holster carrying a loaded .45 Colt revolver; a five-pointed silver star was pinned over the left breast of his long-sleeved cotton shirt. Secure under his left armpit in a leather shoulder holster was another six-shooter. He was taking no chances on this assignment. An Arizona Ranger—a close friend Bill Calhoun—had been murdered here in this dingy, little town a short while ago, and Joaquin had been ordered by Lieutenant Harry Wheeler to investigate the heinous crime, and swiftly bring to justice those responsible. Joaquin's eyes watered and he felt a lump in his throat as he thought of Bill Calhoun.

A strong show of force was needed, according to Wheeler. Four other Rangers, including Wheeler, were due in later in the day. They would assist him in his investigation and patrol the streets for several days, tightening the law enforcement grip on the crime-infested town.

Joaquin wanted desperately to see the crime scene, reportedly in one of the brothels down the street across the railroad tracks. Now was an excellent opportunity to see the room; the saloon wasn't brimming with drunken customers. He continued down the street, leaving behind the Cananea Consolidated Copper Company office and warehouses lining the railroad tracks and the newly constructed $30,000 U.S. customs house, all near the border. He passed the Copper Queen mercantile building, then the solidly-built brick bank along the main one hundred-foot thoroughfare.

Moving quickly as the orange dawn gave way to a clear blue sky, Joaquin changed direction, crossing the railroad tracks as he steadily sauntered up to the *cantina*. Shoving the batwing doors open, he stepped into the darkened interior. He stood to the right of the door just inside, allowing his eyes to adjust. The doors flapped melodiously behind him as he observed an old Mexican man sweeping the floor. *"¿Señor, donde esta su Jefe?* Where's your boss?"

The old man leaned on the broom. His unshaven, weathered face was sunken; white disheveled hair, unkempt clothing and his bent posture told Joaquin of his unlikely future. The man peered intently at the young Ranger's badge before answering. *"Èl no esta aqui, chota. ¿Que quiere?* He's not here, copper. What do you want?"

Joaquin thought a moment. *"Lleveme al cuarto del muerto.* Take me to the room of the dead man."

"¿El cuarto del muerto?" The Mexican stood quietly then nodded his head. *"Sí, Señor. Siguame."* He leaned the broom against the bar, motioned to follow as he walked to the back of the dark room and proceeded slowly up the stairs. Joaquin followed.

The old Mexican stopped at the third door down the hallway, gently opening the unlocked door. He stepped back away from the doorway. Pausing, he stared at the Ranger. *"La puta*—the whore ...*ees dead, tambíen, chota."*

"Yo se. No necisito nada más." Joaquin dismissed the old man as he stepped just inside the room. He stood there, observing the entire room. It was quiet—deathly quiet. Ambient light filtered in through a dirty four-paned window near a small table and an old ragged cot. The dim light undulated before his eyes, floating in layers, and appeared to be suspended in the dense dank air. He shuddered as a cold shiver ran down his neck and arms, then finally down his spine and legs.

Blood stains were still visible on the wooden floor where he stood. Leaning down, he observed someone had half-heartedly scrubbed the wooden plank floor, and remnants of the blood stains still remained. *Two sets of stains near the door?* And a blood streak on the wall to the right of the door behind him.

Joaquin moved cautiously into the room, noticing two additional blood stains—a large-sized one close to the cot and another near the window, adjacent to the wall where the small table was located. He tasted bile in his throat. Swallowing hard, he knelt down between the two scrubbed stains on the floor, looking for anything that may have been left there after the killings, anything at all that seemed out of place.

Finding nothing, Joaquin stood, taking in the entire room. From Wheeler's preliminary information, he knew that Calhoun and the prostitute were both killed as well as the two local thugs Calhoun had shot to death. Calhoun had been working on a case to find who was responsible for the smuggling ring allegedly located in Naco.

A coyote suddenly called out from behind the *can-*

tina; moments passed and several other coyotes answered in unison. Distracted, Joaquin frowned and said out loud, "Damned *coyotes*." Then he shook his head and focused again on the room search.

He lit the kerosene lamp on the small table, held it close to the floor. He shuffled around the entire room, bending forward while he surveyed the room and its contents. *Nothing. There's gotta be something. Nope ... wait a minute ... what's this?* He saw what appeared to be blood on the edge of the small rug. *Or was it?* Joaquin knelt down, setting the lamp on the floor. He reached out, carefully lifting the edge in question. *Yep, it's blood, all right.* He lifted the rug up and away from the floor. His heart pounded in his ears.

Under the rug, someone had attempted to write a message with blood. Joaquin quickly scrambled down on all fours and holding the lamp close; he peered closely at three crude, shaky letters scrawled on the wooden floor. *S ... s ... i ...* what the heck? *It's an "s", "l" or another "s"? Maybe an "i" that's not dotted?* He shook his head slowly, peered closely again at the message and re-confirmed the letters.

What is it, Billy? What are you trying to tell me, amigo? A name ... a location ... *what?* He slammed his palm down hard on the floor, sending dust into the air. "Dammit! What the hell does it all mean?" He let the rug fall back into place as he stood and placed the lamp on the table. Frowning, he pushed his Stetson back on his forehead with his thumb, sighed, and rubbed the rough stubble of two-day old whiskers on his young chin. What *did* it mean?

Removing his hat, he scratched the back of his head as he began to walk around the room. He stopped suddenly in his tracks. *What the ...?* Near the wall behind the door, something caught his eye. He retrieved the lamp again from the table.

Returning, he swung the door closed and knelt

down holding the light out in front of him. He leaned forward. A partial boot heel print was barely discernable in a small pool of dried blood but it definitely was a boot heel. The right boot? *Maybe so.* The rounded portion of the heel was next to the wall. Whoever it was had stood in blood with his back against the wall. *Worn down on the outside with some kind of wooden or metal piece nailed in place to help with the excessive wear.* He'd have to find out if either of the two men Calhoun had shot it out with had worn boot heels.

He straightened, blew out the lamp, and returned the lamp to its original position. As he thought of the clues he had found and their possible significance in assisting him to solve the murder and who was behind the smuggling ring, calmness showed on his troubled face.

Joaquin closed his eyes. He thought of his fellow Ranger. Shot down in the line of duty by a couple of lowdown murdering thugs. *Don't worry, Bill, somehow, someway, I'll figger out what you're tryin' to tell me, and I promise— we'll get every last one of 'em!*

CHAPTER FIVE
Spring, 1906

Carmen Ponce-Campbell leaned over the basket of wet clothing at her feet. She grimaced, straightening as she felt a sharp movement in her swollen abdomen. *The little chiquito is kicking me again—the baby has to be a boy!* No matter, she and Joaquin were so happy that she was with child again. They'd lost the other baby to a miscarriage soon after they were married. It had been devastating for her even though the child had been conceived by rape. Both of them had wanted to raise the child as their own, but it was not to be. *Por Dios.*

The movement subsided. She leaned down, picked up more of the freshly washed clothing, and pinned each article to the clothes line. Peering over the line behind the ranch house and adjacent to Cienega Creek, Carmen was always awed at the sight of the Whetstone Mountains to the east, the bright blue Arizona sky beyond. She had lived here on the ranch all her life, and God help her, she loved it so. Summer was coming on. She felt it already—the hotter, longer days to get necessary ranch work done. Admittedly, she wasn't looking forward to the hot summer and dealing with her pregnancy, but she knew somehow she would get through it all. *Por favor, Dios. Let my baby be born ... and most of all, healthy.*

Carmen bent down, reaching for the clothes basket. She tasted bile in her throat; her stomach was queasy, unsettled, and churning. Dizzy and light-headed, she made her way unsteadily to the shade of a large cottonwood tree, easing herself slowly to the ground. *Don't pass out!* Leaning against the tree, breathing heavily, she fought the nausea and unconsciousness to a standstill. She loosened the collar of her cotton dress, feeling the heavy perspiration on her body. *Joaquin, mi amor. Por favor, come home to me.*

Her father Domingo Ponce and her mother-in-law Marian Campbell were out checking on cattle south of the ranch today. With her father-in-law Lou Campbell dead, shot to death by rustlers two years ago, and her husband still working for the territory as an Arizona Ranger, they all had to pick up the slack and do their part in getting the ranch work done. Their friend Elliott came over frequently from his ranch on the San Pedro River with his new wife Megan and her son Tim. Tim was crippled from polio, but he was a hard worker and very capable in helping with various chores.

Carmen closed her eyes, breathed deeply then exhaled slowly. She began to feel better, her skin not so clammy. She gathered herself and stood, bracing against the big cottonwood tree. Steadying herself, she moved over to the clothesline, gingerly picked up the clothes basket, and shuffled toward the small house she and Joaquin shared together. It was the same house she had been born and raised in. After they had married, her father moved out to the bunkhouse, allowing them much needed privacy. Joaquin's mother, Marian Campbell, resided in the main ranch house.

As Carmen reached the front porch of the little house, she heard a familiar whimper behind her. Smiling, she turned then sat down on the porch. A wooly black and white dog nuzzled her leg.

"Solo Vino!" She petted the old dog's graying head as she looked for her returning husband. "Well, ol' boy, where is he, huh? Where's Joaquin?" Then she saw her husband sitting atop his paint horse, trotting toward the out-buildings of the ranch. He was leading two pack mules. She scratched the old dog behind his ears. He leaned into her, his eyes closed, mouth open, clearly savoring the moment. *Thank you, God. He's home safe and sound. I miss him so when he's gone.*

The paint horse trotted up to the hitch rack in front of the house. "Hi, kiddo!" Joaquin Campbell dropped the reins, grounding his pony as he swung down from the saddle, and tied the lead mule to the hitch rack.

He stepped quickly to where she was seated, and smiling, bent down and kissed her on the cheek. "What are you up to, Carmie?" Looking her over from head to toe, he frowned as he tipped his hat back on his head, "Are you all right? You're not sick, are you?"

She forced a smile for him. "No, I'm fine. Why?"

"You look ... I don't know, pale," He put his arms around her as he sat next to her on the porch.

"I couldn't be better," she replied as he hugged her, kissing her this time on the mouth then again tenderly on her cheek. She thought, *I love you so, Joaquin—always have, always will.*

"Let me put these animals up in the barn, Carmie." He walked to the hitch rack, untied the lead pack mule, and gathered up the loose reins for the paint horse. "Where's Mom and Domingo?"

She responded as he started for the barn. "They're out working south of here today. Checking for any un-branded stock we didn't get in the spring roundup." She hesitated, not wanting to ask. "You ... you'll be home for awhile now, won't you?"

He turned toward her with a painful expression on his face. "I have to head down to Douglas tomor-row—something brewing down south, according to Harry

Wheeler." He cleared his throat, looking down at his feet. She didn't speak, only looked at him, disappointed and sad.

"I'm so sorry, Carmie. I've ... I ... *got* to go," he stammered.

Her face flushed, her dark brown eyes flashing, she said, "You owe the Rangers *nothing*. You hear me? *Nothing!*"

"Carmie—"

"Don't you start! Don't you ... you've served the full year you wanted to with the Rangers and helped bring your father's murderer to justice. Indio Chacon was hung a year and a half ago!" Her face was taut with anger. *"A year and a half ago,* Joaquin. And yet, you ... you stand there and tell me you're still needed in the Arizona Rangers." Tears rolled down her cheeks. Joaquin started toward her. She held out her hands palms up toward him, stamping her foot as she stood, *"No!* No, you go on and put the stock up. Then after supper we'll talk about *us. Our baby. Our lives."*

Joaquin stood motionless, looking at her with sad, knowing eyes. He sighed deeply then turned toward the barn, leading his pony and pack mules.

Carmen felt guilty for what she said to her husband. She truly didn't want to hurt him, but on the other hand she wanted him safe and at home, living and working with them on the ranch. What she didn't want was to become was a thorn in his side, constantly complaining, and causing him to be more stressed than he was already. His work was dangerous, and she knew it was essential for him to focus on his assignments or he could get hurt. She would pray to God for help.

She brushed the tears away as she stepped into the little ranch house, the dog, Solo Vino in tow.

***

Night had fallen. Joaquin lay awake in their small

bed; Carmen snuggled up against his side. Softly, she said, "Resign from the Rangers. *Please.*"

"No, Carmie. They need me to help bring law and order to the territory. I'm making a *real* difference now that I've gained experience as a peace officer." His voice rose, "And we need the extra money to help with the ranch expenses."

She straightened up in bed. "I don't care about the money!"

Joaquin protested, "It's a $100 a month. That's a lot of money, and you know it."

Her voice softened again, "We need you *here*—at home with us."

She won't ever understand what it means to me. I love being a Ranger ... not more than I love her and the baby, though. He honestly didn't know what to do.

"I'm going to Naco in the morning!"

"*Joaquin!*"

"Dammit, Carmie. I'm not quitting the Rangers. That's the end of it."

She sighed deeply, hurt that he had cursed at her and disappointed in his decision. She lay back on her pillow, said nothing.

"I'm sorry. I didn't mean to raise my voice or cuss." When they were first married, his Carmen told him they should *never* go to bed mad nor should he leave home when he was upset. *What can I do?* He wiped at the tears trickling down his face, and then he gently stroked her hair. *I do love you, Carmie. More than life itself.*

Joaquin thought of his dead father. *What would you have me do, Dad?* Swallowing the lump in his throat, he decided he would talk with Elliott, his friend and mentor. The old gunman was always there for him.

CHAPTER SIX
June 1, 1906

It was late in the day on a Friday with the sun just beginning to set as Joaquin Campbell rode into Naco, Arizona. His paint horse trotted up to Hotel Naco. He dismounted stiffly, tied his mount to the hitch rack, and slapped the dust from his clothes. It had been a long day for him, not only the hard riding from the ranch, but also the constant worrying over whether to resign from the Arizona Rangers. He knew fully well that his wife, his mother, and Domingo struggled to get all the work done on the ranch without his help. He and Elliott completed most of the heavy work during roundups in the spring and fall, but there was so much more work to be done throughout the year.

Best shake these thoughts till later—I got work to do. He stepped up on the plank sidewalk and into the hotel lobby.

A familiar voice rang out to him, "Joaquin! How's my special investigator?" Smiling, Lieutenant Harry Wheeler of the Arizona Rangers strode over to him and shook his hand.

Joaquin returned the smile. "I reckon I'm fine, Harry. How 'bout yourself?" He had taken an instant liking to Wheeler: a tough man, a leader of men known to have integrity, courage, and honesty in his repertoire. The slender officer stood five feet four inches tall, and wore a flat-brimmed gray Stetson hat, long-sleeved cotton shirt with buttoned-up cotton vest. High on the left side, a five-pointed silver star displayed, "Arizona Rangers" in the center with "Lieutenant" above it.

"Couldn't be better, son." Wheeler gestured toward several chairs in the corner of the lobby. Both men sat down. Joaquin removed his hat and slapped it against his leg, wishing at once that he hadn't. Dust fell onto the fancy carpet.

Wheeler leaned forward, lowering his voice. "We're checking out your leads in Calhoun's murder case. There's a suspect living right here in Naco who runs one of the dance halls. He's had numerous run-ins with the law before—name's Joe Hansen, but folks around here just call him Slim."

"Slim? You think—"

"It's a possibility, but seems almost too easy. Bill might have been trying to give us a name before he died. Maybe something else." Wheeler shrugged. "Anyhow, we'll keep working on it till we get whoever is responsible for his death. I'd be willing to bet we'll solve his murder when we figure out who's been running guns across the border into Mexico."

"What about the boot heel print?" asked Joaquin.

Wheeler licked his lips, his eyes narrowing "The two men that Calhoun killed weren't wearing boots with the heel built up on the outside. So, the heel print belongs to someone else."

"I'd sure like to help with the case," said Joaquin.

"I figured as much, son. But the case will have to wait for now. A real bad situation has developed down in Cananea, Mexico."

Joaquin frowned. "Why is something happening thirty miles south of the border in Mexico a concern for the Rangers?"

"The Cananea Consolidated Copper Company sent

an urgent telegram today. The message asked for assistance immediately, that American citizens were murdered and property dynamited," returned Wheeler.

"What? Why?"

"Evidently, about 5,000 Mexican miners left the mines down there, congregated in the main plaza. They demanded higher wages, from three to five pesos a day. They wanted an eight-hour day, too." Wheeler settled back in his chair. "Well, Colonel Greene refused their demands, and things took a turn for the worse. The crowd went to the lumberyard where one of the American managers and his brother turned a high-pressure water hose on 'em—the mob allegedly responded by beating and stabbing them to death with miner's candle sticks. Then they set the lumberyard on fire."

Joaquin gasped, "My God."

"That's not the half of it." Wheeler leaned forward in his chair. "There's been violent rioting all day, God only knows what's become of American men, women, and children working and living at the mines."

"What can *we* do? The Mexicans are responsible for enforcement action. Where the hell are Colonel Kosterlitzky and the Rurales?" queried Joaquin.

"They're out fighting the Yaquis who have rebelled—again. Mexican authorities have sent for them, but who knows if they'll arrive in time."

Joaquin thought for a moment. "So, somehow we're going to get mixed up in this ... international affair?"

"I'm afraid so. Captain Rynning has organized about two hundred fifty men in Bisbee, including us. The relief force is made up of Rangers, local peace officers, Rough Riders, and ex-Rangers." Wheeler grinned. "Speaking of ex-Rangers, you'll most likely be pleased to know our old friend Elliott is coming with them on the train tonight."

"Elliott? How did Tom pull that off?"

"He said he sent a rider to the ranch asking Elliott to come help the Rangers and Rough Riders, that he needed his experience and expertise badly for this venture. Elliott dropped what he was doing, strapped on his guns and rode to Bisbee."

"I'm sure glad he'll be with us. It sounds like a damn mess down there," said Joaquin.

Wheeler stood. "Yeah, not to mention the new Governor of the Territory, Governor Kibbey, sent a telegraph advising Tom *not* to enter Mexico under any circumstances."

"What?" Eyebrows raised, Joaquin stood, placing his hat on his head.

"Of course, *officially* we've not seen that telegraph ... most likely won't see it till we get back across the border." Wheeler smiled.

They both heard a train rumbling into the small town—coming from Mexico! Rushing outside the hotel, they saw the train and railroad cars stopped in the vicinity of the administrative offices of the Cananea Consolidated Copper Company just north of the border.

Joaquin's mouth dropped open. The railroad cars didn't contain loaded copper as usual, but literally hundreds of people, mostly women and children. *What the hell?* He and Wheeler walked quickly down to the railroad tracks where everyone was disembarking from the railroad cars. Some women were screaming, others crying; all trying to talk at the same time.

Someone shouted, "Them Messicans is butcherin' Americans down at Cananea!"

"Our men won't be able to hold out much longer. They've got to git help now or it'll be too late," another woman shouted.

Wheeler interjected, "How many have we lost?"

A woman cried out, "Dammit man! They've killed hundreds of us—*hundreds!*"

"Calm down, ma'am. We're Arizona Rangers and here to lead a rescue operation."

Another train arrived in town, adding to the confusion. But this train came in from Bisbee. Joaquin stood watching as several hundred heavily armed men stepped off the railroad cars. The men began to slowly assemble into company formations as assigned officers barked orders into the darkened night. Screams and pleas for help from disembarked passengers echoed out into the darkness, adding to the chaos.

One man stood back from the group, cradling a .30-.40 Winchester rifle in his arms. He wore a battered gray Stetson hat tipped back on his head, displaying a full white mustache and short-cropped white hair against a dark face. Dressed in dusty range clothes, the man looked like any other man there, except the way he wore the old pistol belt and Colt .45 revolver at his side and another six-shooter in an old leather shoulder holster tucked back under his left arm pit. There was a deadly, cold aura about him that made a man take note even in the midst of so many other heavily armed men, made the hair stand up on the back of a man's neck. *Elliott!*

Joaquin's heartbeat quickened. *Thank God. He's made it.*

The old, tall gunman grinned as he strode toward the young Ranger. "*Howdy, mi'jo.* Where's the vittles? I'm plumb wore down to the nub an' half starved, to boot."

CHAPTER SEVEN
Cananea, Mexico-June 2, 1906

The train with its fully loaded rail cars churned and rattled along the railroad tracks south of the Mexican border. Joaquin clutched his .30-.40 1895 Winchester tightly as he sat next to Elliott and other heavily armed men in one of the rail cars headed down the roughly 35 miles of Cananea Consolidated Copper Company-built railway from Naco to Ronquillo, Mexico. *Must be close to mid-day.* The heat was unbearable to the men riding in the open cars. Joaquin wiped at the sweat as it ran in rivulets down his neck, face and into his eyes.

Elliott grinned at Joaquin as he sat in the sweltering heat. He leaned in close. "Hotter'n ten rats in a damn wool sock, ain't it?"

The tenseness and heavy anxiety Joaquin felt earlier faded away, replaced by the sudden urge to laugh out loud. And so he did—loudly, again and again. Elliott joined in the raucous laughter as other nervous men looked on. Within minutes, the entire rail car full of sweating, anxious men roared with laughter as it rolled along through the quiet, still Sonoran desert landscape, startling the Purple Martins and Pygmy owls nesting inside several of the tall saguaro lining the railway.

Governor Rafael Yzabel of the Mexican state of Sonora, along with General Luis Torres, was aboard the train with Captain Tom Rynnning. Yzabel and the general had reluctantly agreed to officially allow the incursion due to exigent circumstances with potential for great loss of life on both sides. He had authorized the 250 men to enter Mexico and advance to Cananea as "volunteers" in the Mexican army. Rynning was conferred the title of Colonel with Harry Wheeler as Lieutenant Colonel in the Mexican army. Fifteen hundred Mexican troops had been dispatched from Mexico City, their arrival at Cananea uncertain.

As the train rumbled southward, Joaquin observed the appearance of the Cananea Mountains in the distance. Later, the rolling, desolate hills appeared close, and he could see Ronquillas, Mexico: an assortment of saloons, dance halls, a large company store and offices, the smelting plant, and meager housing built for the Mexican laborers working various mines at Chivatera, La Democrata, Capote, and several other copper mines located throughout the Cananea Mountains.

The train slid to a halt. The Americans piled out of the railway cars and set up skirmish lines near the tracks, trying to find any available cover or concealment while awaiting further orders. Joaquin ran with Elliott to where some old mining equipment had been left about fifty yards from the tracks. A bullet whined nearby, several ricocheted off the equipment they now hunkered behind.

Elliott's calm voice broke the momentary silence. "'Pears there's a rifle or two up yonder on the mesa, *mijo*. My eyes ain't so good any more. You reckon you could take a quick looksee ... maybe figger out where them boys is sit-i-ated?"

Joaquin swallowed hard, tasting cotton in his parched mouth. He took a deep breath, then darted his head around his cover, just enough to see but not display much of his head. A shot careened off metal near his position, and he saw the glint off the rifle barrel high on the mesa.

"I got one of 'em sighted, Elliott," he shouted, ducking his head back behind cover.

Just then their assigned platoon leader slid in between them. Joaquin had recognized him earlier as one of the local peace officers from Bisbee. The man was perspiring heavily under the hot sun and stress. "We got our orders, boys. Our company will advance up to La Mesa, the American residential district. The other company will be deployed up on the adjacent hill overlooking Ronquillas." He swiped at the sweat running down his face into his eyes and down his thick neck. "And the third company goes to Chivatera Mine. Them Messicans on night shift came out throwing dynamite."

Joaquin recalled Rynning telling him that La Mesa was located on a mesa northeast and above the establishment of Ronquillo. A spur railway led across an arroyo directly in front of them and on up to the top of the mesa where the riflemen were shooting down at them. The platoon leader rose suddenly, waving his arm forward. "Come on men! To the mesa top—*move out!*"

Readying himself, Joaquin crouched to follow his leader as instructed.

"*Don't you move,*" ordered Elliott.

Joaquin hesitated as he watched other men run past his position. Several rifles spoke from above. Two of the men fell to the ground. Another rifle cracked from the mesa. The platoon leader pitched headlong to the railway tracks, a portion of his head blown off.

"Dammit to hell," muttered Elliott as he peered cautiously behind cover. "Damn fool. Had the heart, I reckon. Jest no sense is all." Looking over his shoulder, he yelled out, "Chapo, you an' Pancho git your butts up here when me an' Joaquin start shootin' up at thet *lomita* yonder."

Chapo Carter and Frank Shaw, fellow Rangers from the former Douglas squad crouched near an abandoned railway car behind them. Carter, an old cowpuncher and Rough Rider, who had enlisted in the Arizona Rangers in 1901 alongside Elliott, spat tobacco out the side of his mouth. "Whenever you're ready, you ol' fart." He spat again. "What the hell are you doin' here anyways? I thought you was *re*-tired, *pedo*."

"I am *re*-tired, you bow-legged, banty rooster!" shouted Elliott back over his shoulder. He scooted around for a better firing position. Joaquin did the same on the opposite side of their cover. "Your shot come from them bushes on the ridge line, boy?"

"Yessir," said Joaquin.

"*Bueno, mi'jo*. There's another rifle at thet boulder 'bout 50 yards to the left o' yours. On the count o' three."

Joaquin left both eyes open as he squinted through the adjustable sights on his .30-.40 Winchester, applying gentle pressure on the trigger as he counted. His first shot surprised him. Hearing Elliott's second shot, he fired again, and again, at last hearing and feeling the two other Rangers slide in safely next to them behind cover. He automatically filled the box magazine to capacity with five rounds and ensured that a round was loaded in the chamber.

Elliott was talking. "You boys give me an' Joaquin cover fire whilst we move up to them boulders yonder next to the railroad trestle."

"Thet there is a fur piece to run, *viejo*. You reckon you're up to it? Chapo grinned broadly at his former boss.

"Yessir, I reckon so," drawled Elliott. "You fellers see where we was a shootin'?"

"Yep." Carter said. He and Shaw moved into shooting positions.

Joaquin took a quick drink of water from the canteen slung over his shoulders and grasped his rifle tightly. The hot water did not taste good. *Hell, at least it's wet.* He took a deep breath, readying himself before the shooting commenced.

Run! Run, like the wind. Zig zag. Like Elliott showed you. Joaquin ran toward the trestle, the canteen pounding his back with every bound. Leaping over one of the downed Americans, he saw peripherally that Elliott was just a step or two behind him to his left. Carter and Shaw were laying down steady cover fire. Finally, he crossed the trestle, rounded a curve, and saw a small railway building.

Elliott stumbled then recovered without falling, and swore out loud. Joaquin had forgotten about the old gunman's knee that had been shot up in the Spanish-American War. He kneeled and fired. On he ran, then dove in behind the small building. Bullets splattered the desert sand behind him where he had knelt just seconds before. Several rounds slammed into the building near where he lay panting now that the cover fire had stopped. Gasping for breath, he brought his rifle to bear on his former target on the mesa top.

***

Pain stabbed through Elliott's right knee and up along his thigh. Wincing, he ran quickly across the railroad bridge behind Joaquin. *I'm way too damn old fer this. Gawd, please give me the strength to keep up with the boy. I swore to Megan thet I'd see him get outta this here scrape.*

His knee hurt almost unbearably, but he was somehow able to keep moving, ascending the mesa after crossing the small bridge. No shots at them so far. The other Rangers were continuing cover fire from the other side of the bridge, but each man only had six rounds in his rifle before he would need to reload. Elliott gritted his teeth, breathing heavily. *Run, damn you! You're losing ground behind the boy.*

He rounded a curve in the tracks, saw Joaquin stop ahead of him, kneel and squeeze off a shot to the right. Limping badly, but still running, Elliott saw a man with a rifle pitch forward to the ground. Joaquin was up and running toward the small railway station on top of the mesa another hundred yards distant down the tracks. *Good boy! Keep movin'.* They were both out in the open.

Their cover fire ceased momentarily. *Dammit!* Elliott's breathing was ragged now, the muscles in his legs weak. He began to falter, his chest burned, the pain in his knee excruciating. Joaquin had made it to the railway terminal building and was kneeling behind it with his rifle aimed on a target to the east. Joaquin's rifle spoke, rising slightly. Another shot. *Jeez, only fifty feet more.* A bullet hit the ground in front of Elliott. Sand flew up into the air. *Zeu ..uit!* Another round hit behind him as he struggled the remaining distance to cover and safety.

Joaquin's rifle cracked again. And again. Clenching his teeth, Elliott threw his rifle ahead of him as he summoned all his remaining strength and dove in behind the young Ranger.

He lay in the hot sand, the heat of the day bearing down unmercifully on him. He had lost his hat as he pitched headlong. Perspiration poured down his face, his neck. His burning chest heaved as he struggled for a decent breath of fresh air. His ears pounded. Someone was talking.

"Elliott ... you ... all right?"

A firm hand shook him, gently at first, then with no response, more roughly. "You're not hit are you?" asked Joaquin urgently.

Elliott swallowed hard, tasting sand in his parched mouth, pushed himself up to a sitting position against the shed. "No ... don't reckon I'm hit, *mi'jo*. Jest ... plumb ... wore down ... to the nub," he gasped.

"I shot one of 'em." Joaquin peered around the corner of the shed. "It looked as if the other'n was running away toward the houses. Not sure though."

Finally getting his breath back, Elliott reached out and patted the young Ranger on the back. "Ya done good, boy." He placed the old weather-beaten Stetson on his head, picked up his rifle with one hand and rubbed his throbbing knee with the other.

"We got to make shore they've gone, then cover Chapo, Pancho, and the rest of the troops whilst they git their tails on up here." He thought for a moment, peering around the building at the previous locations of the two snipers. "You all right with me coverin' ya to them boulders o'er yonder?"

"Sure. What about the man on the ground I shot?" asked Joaquin.

Elliott's blue eyes were hard. "Shoot 'im agin when you pass 'im," he rasped between clenched teeth.

Joaquin stood, reloaded the rifle's box magazine. He started to leave the shed then turned back toward his mentor. "Elliott ... I ... I can't ... *do* that." His tongue played with the inside of his cheek. "It was different when he was trying to *kill me.*"

Elliott's piercing blue eyes softened as he peered at the young Ranger. "You're right *not* to do it, *mijo*. I shouldn't've told ya thet." Sighing deeply, he said, "Sometimes, I ... drop back to my killin' ways." He hesitated, pulling on the corners of his mustache. "There was a time ... I reckon when I killed jest 'bout ever'thing. Ain't somethin' I'm proud of, boy." Elliott shuffled around to an adequate shooting position to cover Joaquin. "Jest take his rifle when you pass 'im by, *mijo*," he said out of the corner of his mouth as he brought the Winchester up to eye level.

CHAPTER EIGHT
La Mesa Residential Area, Mexico

lliott and Joaquin secured the mesa top above Ronquillas then provided cover for the remainder of their company ascending up to the heights. Tom Rynning and Harry Wheeler arrived and accompanied them as they moved cautiously into the American residential area.

Joaquin heard sporadic firing in the distance. He strode forward, his rifle at the ready. Rynning had assigned Elliott as the new platoon leader and their platoon to take point as the entire company advanced. They passed several empty houses and two American men's bodies sprawled nearby. One of the men had been shot in the chest; the other had been bludgeoned to death, his face almost unrecognizable.

A flimsy wooden shack came into view. Several American women were sitting out on the porch waving at them.

Rynning returned the wave. "Get back inside! Where it's safer for you." One of the women laughed loudly, "Hell, we're as safe outside as inside with these hyar thin walls. Them goddamn rifle bullets go right through 'em." She giggled, looked at Rynning. "When you boys git through with them goddamned greasers, you come on back o'er here, uh?" Another woman laughed and said, "We'll be a waitin' fer ya."

Joaquin looked at the women as he strode past. *Boy,*

they look like a rough bunch. He couldn't ever remember hearing women swear like that.

They advanced farther into the housing area without any more casualties. Several Mexicans fired at them, then quickly retreated in the face of the superior armed force of disciplined men. The sound of rapid rifle fire suddenly ripped through the quiet of the afternoon. Joaquin ducked behind one of the dilapidated houses.

Elliott appeared beside him, taking a quick look around the corner of the house. "Looks like we almost made it to Colonel Greene's mansion, *mijo.*"

Joaquin knew their company's main objective was to reinforce the Americans forted up at the mansion. According to information from the survivors, most of the women and children who hadn't escaped by railway were still inside. Dave Allison, head of security for the mine, had made his stand there. Most of the Arizona Rangers knew Allison well for he had served with distinction as a Ranger during 1901-02, leaving for a higher paying job. The $50,000 sprawling, elegant mansion was well known throughout the territory. It had been built in 1902, and it was rumored to include stables and a sunken Italian garden.

Elliott interrupted his thoughts. "Rynning wants us to move on in. Clear them bastards out as we go." He checked his rifle; it was fully loaded. Looking at Joaquin, he placed his hand on the young Ranger's shoulder. "You be careful now. There'll be snipers. You won't see 'em, jest hear the shot, or feel the hit if you're the unlucky target."

He grasped the boy's shoulder tightly, peering intently at him. "Use your cover, a bush, anything, to keep some sumbitch from getting' a clean shot at ya."

"Yessir." Joaquin took a drink of hot water from his canteen. He removed his dusty brown Stetson and poured water over his head, wetting it.

The platoon spread out as they moved cautiously forward toward the mansion. Elliott walked out at the point of their "V" formation. Joaquin was next to the old Ranger with the veteran Chapo Carter to his right, Frank Shaw to the left of Elliott. An eerie silence ensued as they advanced; the large mansion appeared even more immense to Joaquin.

Carter whirled quickly to his left, bringing his Spanish Mauser rifle to his shoulder. The rifle cracked, the silence broken. Joaquin saw a man fall from a rooftop, his rifle clattering against the building as it too fell to the street below. Another shot rang out. The hot round sizzled past Joaquin's left ear. He felt raw fear deep inside his belly. *Oh, my God!*

He turned quickly toward the threat, bringing his rifle up to his shoulder. *Thwack!* Another bullet slammed into his supporting hand, knocking the rifle away from his grasp. In slow motion, he saw the rifle spinning, end over end. Blood erupted from his left hand. A numbing pain. He stood there, stunned, wanting somehow to reach out and grasp his rifle and his injured hand. Instinctively, he knelt instead, and drew his .45 revolver.

A loud report from a rifle. Another round passed directly overhead where he had been standing and slammed into the ground nearby. He heard Elliott's rifle crack and the old Ranger yelling at him, but he couldn't make it out. Most of the platoon was running hard toward the cover of the mansion, others providing covering fire. Elliott grabbed his elbow and pushed him along as he ran.

A figure rose out from behind the corner of a building, then another. Joaquin's heart pounded in his chest. *They're close!* Joaquin broke from Elliott's embrace and knelt, bringing his revolver up as he cocked the single-action six-shooter. *Blam!* The big pistol bucked in his hand

and the man clutched his chest. Peripherally, he saw Elliott throw his rifle to the ground and swiftly draw his six-shooter. Flame and lead belched from the barrel as the old gunman turned slightly, fanning the hammer again, and again. Joaquin saw two men, then another fall to the ground.

Elliott holstered an empty pistol, drawing the other encased in the shoulder holster under his left arm pit. He cocked it as he reached down and helped Joaquin to his feet. "Run *mijo. Run*! I'll cover ya."

Joaquin hesitated.

"Are ya deef, boy? *Run, dammit* or we'll both be killed out here in the open!"

Joaquin turned and ran hard, zigzagging toward the mansion nearly fifty yards distant. He heard the old gunman's .45 blazing away behind him.

***

The large living room inside Greene's mansion smelled of gun smoke, blood, and death; an occasional shot resounded loudly in the cavernous interior. Elliott heard several children crying, the smaller ones loudly, the older ones silently. *This here's a damn bad sit-i-a-tion fer shore.* He watched with anxiety as one of the women bandaged Joaquin's injured left hand. Joaquin had lost most of his little finger and the top portion of his ring finger. His hand and other fingers did not appear to be affected, but the young Ranger was in a lot of pain.

Elliott handed him a piece of leather he had found in his saddle bag for repairing tack. "Put this in your mouth and bite down on it, *mijo*." As he placed it between Joaquin's teeth, he felt the boy quiver, shake, then swallow hard from the excruciating pain.

Just then Dave Allison shouted, "Riders comin' in a shootin', boys!"

Moving to an open window, Elliott peered out and saw a long column of riders trotting toward them, shooting as they advanced toward the mansion. He saw a stout man with a black mustache mounted on a white horse at the head of the column. He wore a large sombrero; the men all wore the silver trimmed gray charro uniforms. The man was shouting commands to the other men. *Kosterlitzky!*

"Dave, it's the Rurales with Colonel Kosterlitzky! Don't shoot at 'em. They're on our side," shouted Elliott.

He heard Allison yell, "The Rurales have finally arrived, boys. Cease fire!"

Elliott looked again at Joaquin; the young Ranger was trying his best to form a big smile for him. He heard horses' shod hooves clattering on the cobblestone sidewalks outside the mansion and Captain Tom Rynning's voice, "It's good to see you, Emilio."

Kosterlitzky's spurs rattled as he dismounted. "Just what the hell are you *gringos* doing in Mexico?" he demanded.

"Easy, *amigo*. No one could reach you and the situation demanded immediate action. Hell, we would've had uncontrolled bands of armed men pouring across the border if I hadn't acted with Governor Yzabel," said Rynning.

Yzabel interjected, *"Es la verdad, Emilio."*

The Colonel turned to another Rurale officer and said in Spanish, "Martial law is now declared. Anyone who resists you is to be shot, the leaders of this insurrection arrested. Then *I* will judge their fate." He motioned curtly for the man to get moving.

Elliott thought, *'dobe-walled, I reckon.* Numerous times over the years, he had seen the Rurales line prisoners up along the adobe-walled buildings and shoot them. His memory of the blood-stained walls and the wailing of loved ones left behind had always tainted his working experiences with the Rurales. *I reckon it's a hard world thet we live in.*

Turning to Tom Rynning, Kosterlitzky bowed. "I apologize for my outburst, *Capitán*. But of course you and Rafael were correct in your decision." A cruel smile formed. "However, your admirable services are no longer required." He paused, pulling at the black mustache, and said to Governor Yzabel, "I think it appropriate that these armed Americans leave Mexico first thing in the morning. Don't you agree, Rafael?"

"*Si, Coronel. Tienes razon.*"

"Whatever we can do to assist till morning, Emilio." returned Rynning easily.

Kosterlitzky bowed again, smiling broadly as he now considered himself in full control. "*Gracias, Capitán. Muchas gracias.*" Then he looked around, his eyes searching. "Where's that damned Elliott son-of-a-beech? I hear he's been killing all these bandit *cabrones*." This time his white teeth were displayed in a genuine smile.

CHAPTER NINE
Spring, 1907

Elliott slowly walked from the barn carrying a bucket of axle grease with Tim Campbell in tow, allowing the boy to keep pace as they headed for the windmill. He set the battered old bucket down and secured the windmill from pivoting in the wind with a rusty number nine telephone wire that was secured to the windmill tower. Too damn many good cowpunchers forgot to secure a windmill and were swept off the platform to their deaths.

The boy spoke, "Elliott, you ... ever take a special ... liking to a girl? You know ... when you were in school?"

Surprised at the question, Elliott turned to Timmy leaning forward on his crutches. "I reckon I've not had much schoolin', *mi'jo*, but I've shore been known to take a *real* liking to gals o'er the years." Smiling, he placed his hand on Timmy's head, looking into his eyes. "It's a shore 'nough natural thing fer boys to do when they git to your age. Why? You got some lil' filly thet's got your blood running hot?" He laughed out loud.

"Wel-l-l. I ... I really like Kelly an awful lot ... she sits next to me in school. She's so pretty ... and nice, too! But ..."

"But ..." Elliott continued for him, his piercing blue eyes searching the boy's face. "You ain't so shore she feels the same way 'bout you, 'cause you're crippled an' sech." He paused, watching Timmy's face. "Thet 'bout it, in a nutshell?"

The boy looked down, sighed, and nodded. "Yes sir. I guess that's about the way it is." He looked up into the older man's eyes. "Will I *always* be thinking this way, Elliott?"

Elliott placed his hands on the boy's shoulders. "When you care 'bout someone—really, *truly* care it always matters to ya if they don't feel the same way as you." He ruffled the boy's disheveled hair. "But remember this, *mi'jo*, you got to be *yourself*, an' to hell with the rest o' it. If a body don't love ya fer what you are—lock, stock, an' barrel—why, they ain't worth the effort, I'd say."

Timmy's face brightened. "Do you think I could ask her to come out and visit us some time?"

"Why shore. Jest any time would be fine. Meg and I'd like to meet her. She sounds like a real fine girl. I always said you was a good judge o' character, boy." Elliott turned toward the windmill. "We'll go get her, her Mom and Daddy if need be. The whole kit an' caboodle. You jest give me the word."

Timmy smiled, "Thank you."

"De nada, mi'jo."

Ascending the rickety ladder to the small wooden platform near the top, Elliott pulled a cotton rope from his shoulders and secured it to his waist, then to the windmill platform.

He looked out over the countryside from his vantage point. The Arizona sky was a bright-blue with all the cottonwood trees displaying lush green foliage that undulated in the morning breeze. Elliott grunted as he watched the trees. *Damn near makes a man ready fer a nap. Reckon I got too much work to get done though.*

Looking southward, he could barely make out some of the outbuildings of the community of St. David. Mormon folks lived there, different somewhat in religious beliefs, but no matter to him. They were some of the finest men and women he had the pleasure of knowing in his troubled, violent life. Hard workers and good, honest friends to him—strong family folks.

A man could believe in God, or not, he reckoned; some folks were mighty particular in their beliefs on religion and refused to have anything to do with others of a different faith. Honestly, he believed in God, but he had no truck with someone who disagreed with him on how to worship. He had joined the Catholic faith when he married his first wife, and he figgered on staying with 'em whenever he took the notion to go to church.

The country was changing, that was for sure; somehow though, the past had always remained for him, living and breathing along side him as he toiled on his small ranch. The old voices whispered softly to him as a gentle breeze might caress a man's cheek. It had not been all that long ago when the feared Apache ruthlessly ruled the countryside, raiding where they pleased, taking whatever they wanted with no one capable of stopping them.

Elliott smiled, his dark weather-beaten face wrinkling in the sunlight, as he thought of the time he first brought his young, beautiful wife to this very spot—their ranch—an opportunity to make something meaningful out of life. Together, they had worked hard building the house, the barn, slowly expanding his cow-calf operation. They were so happy just being together, loving each other, and making an honest living from the land. His son Joaquin was born, and Elliott thought he surely didn't deserve all the blessings bestowed upon him at that time in his young life.

Then one day when he was away from the ranch, the Apache came. They raped and murdered his wife, and then almost in afterthought as they were leaving, they bashed his son's small head against a rock. Sadly, that day had forever changed his life, his personal demeanor, his whole attitude toward life. His killing of the four warriors responsible for the atrocities did not appease him; it only further fueled this hatred and bitterness toward the Apache and his urgent longing for his own impending death. *Strange how life works out sometimes.*

A soft voice called out to him. "Elliott, do you want this bucket up there?"

He peered down at the young twelve-year old boy sitting on the ground below. "Shore thing, *mijo*. Tie this here rope on it like I showed you—a square knot, not no granny, ya hear?" He tossed the remaining cotton rope down to the boy.

Timmy Campbell deftly caught the rope and secured it to the bucket's bail with a perfect square knot. He shouted up that it was secure as he scrambled out from beneath the bucket's intended path.

Elliott pulled the bucket up and onto the platform, feeling the breeze pull at his sweat-stained gray Stetson. He liberally greased the gears in the gear box, taking his time. It was better to do it right this time and not have to get back up on the rickety ladder and small platform again for awhile. *This ain't much o' a place fer a gimpy ol' man.* As he used a rag from his back pocket to remove the grease from his hands, he thought he caught a glint in the bright sunlight—a reflection near the tree-line south of the ranch? He paused in cleaning his hands, and squinted. Nothing. *My ol' eyes are playin' tricks on me agin.* As he finished wiping his hands clean of grease, he shouted that he was sending the bucket back down. Slowly, he began to lower it to the boy below.

Suddenly, his peripheral vision caught movement, this time to the west of the ranch house. *What the hell? Someone circlin' the place?* For the first time in a long while, he had a bad feeling in the pit of his stomach. He spoke quietly to the young boy below, "Timmy, my good friend. You reckon you kin fetch my gun belt thet's hanging on a peg by the front door?"

The boy stood, using his crutches to support his weight. "You reckon to let me practice shooting again, Dad?" He smiled up at the old Ranger.

"Maybeso. Right now, we've got us company comin' an' they're bein' mighty sneaky an' *lowdown* 'bout it."

Elliott saw a bay horse, then a black hat, then nothing in the thick canopy of the cottonwood trees lining the San Pedro River northwest of the ranch headquarters. His tongue played with one side of his white mustache, then the other side. He called out to the retreating boy without breaking eye contact with the terrain, "Hustle now, Timmy ... see if you kin git thet pistol to me quick-like."

Tim Campbell looked up at Elliott, the beginnings of fear showing in his eyes. He said nothing, turned and walked as fast as he could with his wooden crutches toward the house. Almost falling at the porch, he crawled up the steps, leaving his crutches behind.

Elliott untied the rope securing him to the windmill and climbed down. Walking to the ranch house porch, he wiped his hands again, this time on his faded blue work shirt. He sat down heavily on the porch steps while scanning the terrain where he instinctively knew the rider would approach the house. He heard movement behind him on the porch, but did not turn nor take his eyes off his intended field of vision. Feeling the gun belt pressed into his back, he gripped it in his right hand and stood, bringing the belt around him as he did so. As he buckled the heavy belt around his waist, he watched a bay horse and rider break from the tree line heading directly toward him.

"Thank ya, Timmy. I reckon I kin always depend on

you, *mijo*."

The horse and rider came on. "Do you want me to get the rifle, Elliott?" There was fear in the young boy's trembling voice, but determination there as well.

Elliott's grim face softened. He spoke softly, "No, I reckon not, Timmy. You jest set inside fer a spell." He pursed his lips. *We'll jest see what this sumbitch is up to.* He moved slightly so the sun was mostly at his back, and stood squarely, his right hand and arm hanging near the old, weathered holster with the brown butt of the Colt .45 halfway between his elbow and his wrist. That bad feeling in the pit of his stomach returned.

The spirited bay horse pranced sideways while being held in check by his rider. Horse and rider stopped within forty feet of Elliott. The man wore a black hat, the hat band interlaced with small silver conchos. The face beneath the flat brim was young, yet with hard features that seemed somehow out of place on a youthful face. The man's eyes were small, piercing, a dull green color.

Something about the man seemed out of place to Elliott. Suddenly, he realized the man's face was a pale, white pallor—not the complexion of someone accustomed to being out-of-doors. The man stared at Elliott for a moment while sitting atop his horse, taking in Elliott's armed presence, position in relation to the bright sun, the grease-stained face and work shirt, and lastly the wooden crutches lying on the ground near the steps of the ranch house.

The man dismounted slowly while maintaining his eye contact with Elliott, holding on to his saddle horn and the bay horse's mane. Ever so slowly, cat-like, he eased to the ground, and as his left boot slipped from the stirrup, he moved cautiously but deliberately to ensure that he was not facing directly into the sun. Still seemingly uncomfortable with this new position, he started to move again.

Elliott's voice crackled in the morning air. "Thet's fer enough!" His voice had a metallic ring to it. "You move agin, I'll kill ya."

The man hesitated, shrugged. "I mean you no harm ... leastways ... not today." A cocky, quick smile formed on thin lips. Slowly, he moved his hands up to shoulder level. With his eyebrows raised, he said, "You Elliott?" The question hung in the air, unanswered.

The man wore a black vest neatly buttoned up with a gold watch chain running from one pocket of the vest to another on the other side. He wore two pearl-handle six-guns in holsters attached to a black polished pistol belt. Both holsters were tied down to his legs. His black pants were tucked into expensive high-top boots. *Hells bells, the white-livered sumbitch is even wearin' black gloves.*

"I just want to talk with you, Elliott. I'm Slydell Coburn. Maybe you've heard of *me*?" The small eyes decreased in size, a twitch appeared on the right side of the man's face.

"Nope." The metallic ring was still there.

"My boss asked me to come out here and make you ... an offer you couldn't refuse." Coburn licked his dry, cracked lips.

"He tell ya to come straight in, like a man, or sneak around like some *low down* yeller dog?"

The man's confident demeanor changed, his lip curled, the small eyes hardened, blazing. "Nobody talks to me that way, *you* goddamned old *bastard*," he said through clenched teeth.

Elliott's face showed a fleeting smile then it vanished. "Who was it sent ya?"

"Ben Hyde."

Ben Hyde? The name immediately invoked memories of Elliott's dark past. The last Elliott recalled of Hyde was that he headquartered out of Naco, spent a lot of time down in Mexico and was involved in anything illegal that made him easy money. Hyde had hired him to kill three rival competitors who were hiding in Mexico at the time. Sanchez, Sandoval, and Simon—*Las Tres Viberas*—The Three Snakes, Hyde had called them. *Jeez, thet was years ago. An' shore ain't nothin' to be proud of on my part.* When Elliott killed those men he had felt no remorse, no nagging conscience. Nothing. They had been bad men—bandits, criminals, who had murdered many others less fortunate or capable. After the killings, Hyde triumphantly had a tattoo placed on his own forearm commemorating the event.

"Mister Hyde has a business proposition for you," Coburn said.

"I'm listenin'."

"He, uh, *we* need your help in moving certain ... goods across the border into Mexico." Coburn paused, licking his thin lips. "He said you were the best gun hand he ever saw—a real killin' machine." He licked his lips again. "He said you was in the fight at the Middleton Ranch in Pleasant Valley back in '87 standin' with Jim Tewksbury." Coburn licked hard at the saliva formed on his lower lip, his green eyes brightened. "That you was the one what blowed Hampton Blevins brains out and then killed John Paine."

Elliott let the air slowly out of his lungs. He clearly remembered that hot, August day long ago standing beside Tewksbury as Jim told the five cowboys from the Graham faction who had ridden up arrogantly asking for dinner, "No sir, we don't keep a hotel here."

"Why me? Why now?"

"Mister Hyde heard you left the Rangers, and uh, they've been giving us some trouble lately—*you know* in conducting business across the border."

"Good fer 'em," returned Elliott.

Coburn's face turned ugly again. "Don't get smart with me!"

"I reckon I'll do as I please. Mister *Slydell* Coburn." Elliott's piercing, blue eyes bored into Coburn.

"Don't be a fool! Mister Hyde don't take kindly taking "*no*" for an answer."

"He'd best git used to it. If I help anybody, it'll be the Rangers—not your boss," said Elliott evenly.

Coburn slowly dropped his hands to his side. A smirk appeared at the corners of his mouth. "You're a bigger fool than I thought you'd be, and a helluva lot older." He moved his left hand, motioning toward the house; the right hand hovered over the six-gun at his hip. "You'd best think of the woman, the chink, and that boy's safety. *Hell, look at ya.* You're nothin' but a used-up *old* man living in a shit-hole place." Hesitating, his voice pleaded, "Think about it—you have a chance to make some *big* money, live high on the hog."

"I have. An' I ain't interested," answered Elliott.

Coburn's hands moved closer to his tied-down guns. "I could *kill* you. Here an' now."

"Maybeso." Elliott sighed. "But somehow, I reckon not."

"No?"

"I'm plumb tired o' you, mister. Either pull them pistols or *git!*" The metallic ring was back in his voice.

His face contorted with rage, Coburn flexed the fingers in both hands, staring hard at Elliott. His eyes were pointed, full of seething hatred. He turned sharply, mounted his horse and rode back the way he had come.

Elliott watched the man disappear into the thick, green foliage near the river. *Thet's a mighty dangerous feller— a killer.* He exhaled sharply. *Was I like him back in them ol' days?* He reached in his pants pocket and withdrew the old brown wood rosary Father Ramon Quinones had given him years ago. *I plumb forgot to pray this mornin', Maria.*

A soft voice interrupted his dark thoughts. "I don't think I like that man very much." Tim Campbell sat just inside the house behind the screen door. He clutched El-liott's rifle tightly in his small hands.

CHAPTER TEN

It was spring—planting time. The sun warmed Megan Elliott's back as she finished planting the chunk of potato in the moist brown dirt. She had dug the hole to the desired depth, placed the correct portion of dried cow manure in, covered it with dirt and planted the "eye" on top before scooping in the top layer of moist soil. She wiped her soft brown hair back from her forehead, trying not to smear it with dirt and peered inside the gunny sack lying on the ground beside her. Five left to plant. Sitting back on her heels in the tilled soil, she watched Hao Li plant corn in a straight row designated by a taut piece of twine tied between two stakes.

The old Chinaman moved effortlessly in the garden. She reflected that one hardly noticed he was there; he was so quiet, unassuming. When he did speak, which was rare, his tone was again quiet, almost soft. She knew he thought highly of Elliott and had grown to love the entire family. *What a wonderful man and friend.* He had helped Elliott regain his life many years ago when he had hit rock-bottom, and the old Ranger had never forgotten his debt to the Chinaman who was several years older than he.

Two days prior, Megan and Hao Li had traveled together to the Campbell Ranch on Cienega Creek to help the Campbells, leaving Elliott and Tim to complete the daily ranch chores at Elliott's ranch. A productive garden was essential for ranch survival, and no one was better than the old Chinaman to ensure copious yields of vegetables.

Potatoes, tomatoes, beans and squash as well as corn, beets, radish, and lettuce were needed to sustain Megan's mother, Domingo Ponce, Carmen's father, and of course her brother Joaquin and his wife, Carmen.

The family ate fresh vegetables when ready for harvest, but canned the majority to supplement the beef, pork, and chicken meat available on the ranch. Megan reached inside the gunny sack for another potato "eye". She hesitated as she heard a baby cry out behind her. Turning toward the porch of the ranch house, she saw Carmen sitting on the porch; lift her baby while supporting its head, placing it next to her unbuttoned blouse. The baby boy immediately found her breast and began suckling. Megan chuckled, recalling her own son's uncanny ability to always find the food source.

A hand touched her shoulder. She looked up to see Joaquin standing beside her. He looked longingly at his wife and son on the porch and then smiled at her. "Come on, sis. Let's get some lunch and take a break from all this sodbuster work, huh?"

He helped her up with his right hand, holding the injured left hand behind him out of sight.

"Why, thank you, Joaquin. I am somewhat hungry," she said.

Joaquin hollered at Hao Li, and the three of them headed toward the old ranch house that sat under several large cottonwood trees about a hundred yards from Cienega Creek. A slight breeze stirred the green canopy of the trees and tugged gently at Megan's hair. *Joaquin is so self-conscious of his injured hand.* She shuddered at the thought of her brother being shot. So close to death. She thanked God every day that the injury had not been more severe—that he or Elliott had not been killed at Cananea. She had truly not wanted Elliott to go when he had been asked to return

and assist the Rangers, but she felt somewhat selfishly relieved knowing that Elliott would be there for her brother.

Joaquin hadn't talked about the injury since returning home. The hand had pretty much healed, but he always
placed his left hand conveniently in a pocket or behind
him, out of sight. When Elliott and Joaquin returned from
Mexico, her husband had cautioned, "Leave 'im be, Meg. I
reckon he'll git o'er it in his own good time."

Megan knew somehow he would, but she could not
help agonizing for him when she saw him struggling. And
then there was the tension between him and Carmen over
his decision to remain with the Rangers. Megan sighed as
she approached the porch and sat down next to Carmen
and the baby. He had been born while Joaquin was working
away from home—in Mexico—yet another point of con-
tention for the young couple.

"How are you and little Lou doing, Carmen?" she
asked.

Carmen smiled at her friend. "*Muy bien, gracias,*
Meg."

The baby boy butted his head at his mother's breast,
continuing to feed with a contented look on his face. Joaquin sat next to his wife. He leaned in and kissed her on
the cheek then touched his son gently with his right hand.
"He's a good lookin' lil' feller, huh?"

Carmen smiled at him, her sad brown eyes convey-
ing her love for him. "*Sí.* He looks like his father."

"Naw ... lil' Lou looks more like his grandpa every
day, I'd say," returned Joaquin. He turned to his sister. "How
did Elliott's birthday party come out anyhow?"

Megan smiled broadly. "He really liked his pocket
watch, Joaquin."

"What did he say when he opened the box?"

"Those blue eyes just sparkled."

"I'll bet," Joaquin said, "But what did he *say?*"

Megan thought for a moment. "He looked real close at the watch, turning it over in his hands. You know, kinda inspecting it."

"And ...?" Joaquin pressed his sister, his eyebrows raised, chewing on his lip.

"Then he said, 'Yessir. I reckon it's four *O*-clock by this here handy-dandy, brand-spankin' new watch. Thank ya—all o' ya.'"

Joaquin and Carmen laughed out loud, thinking of the old Ranger and his peculiar manner of speech. They had all pitched in money to purchase him the gold watch for his fifty-seventh birthday.

Megan leaned forward on the porch. "Joaquin, what's happening with the Rangers?" He didn't respond right away. She hesitated. "Do you have to go back to work soon?"

Looking down at his dusty boots, Joaquin remained silent for several minutes. He leaned forward with his elbows resting on his thighs. "Cap'n Rynning was summoned to Phoenix by Governor Kibbey after the Cananea incident. They say in the newspapers that we started an international incident when we went down there armed to the teeth. The governor, he was real mad at Tom especially since he had sent telegrams ordering us *not* to go on down there." He looked out toward the newly planted garden. "Diaz booted Governor Yzabel out for appointing us "volunteers" in the Mexican Army and allowing us to go into Mexico. And Governor Kibbey gave Tom the boot—he's not our Captain anymore."

"Fired him?" Megan queried.

"Yeah. Only he made it look kinda okay by appointing him Superintendent at Yuma Territorial Prison." Joaquin licked his dry lips. "Sergeant Hopkins down at the

Douglas station resigned when he heard about Tom."

"That's a real loss for the Rangers. I've always liked Tom and Arthur. What did President Roosevelt say about your armed incursion across the border?" asked Megan.

"Ol' Teddy didn't have much to say I guess—just, 'Well, Tom's all right, isn't he?'" Joaquin grunted, and then laughed. Roosevelt and Rynning had served together as Rough Riders in Cuba and were close friends.

Joaquin stood, shuffling his boots. "I have to ride to Naco tomorrow." He looked at Carmen, noticed the smile fade on her face, the sad brown eyes take on new meaning. Letting the air out of his lungs, he placed both hands in his back pockets. "I've got to talk to a suspect with Harry Wheeler about Bill Calhoun's murder." He kicked at the ground with the toe of his boot. "Harry's our new Captain now, did I tell you?"

"No. Is that a good choice?" asked Megan. Carmen remained silent, a frown on her pretty, brown face.

A deeping frown appeared on Carmen's face. "I believe he'll make a good leader for us. Elliott has always thought highly of him."

Marian Campbell appeared on the porch and waved everyone into the old ranch house. "Come on in an' have somethin' to eat, ya'll."

***

Joaquin noticed his mother's hair was almost completely white; her lined face haggard, drawn in the full sunlight of mid-day. *Carmen's right. I need to be here to help with the ranch.* Domingo was aging as well, fully capable of a hard day's work, but feeling his age at the end of the day. *Should I leave the Rangers? God, I just don't know what to do! They need me, too, and we need the extra money to keep the ranch afloat.*

As everyone filed up the steps and into the house, Joaquin stood silently then called out, "I'll be right in." He had a difficult time swallowing the lump in his throat. Something nudged his leg. He ignored it. Then another nudge. Joaquin looked down at his friend, Solo Vino. The old dog's eyes shone as he peered up at his master, his mouth open and tongue out, tail wagging.

Joaquin's dark thoughts disappeared. He smiled at his companion, reached down and patted the dog's head. Solo Vino moved in closer to him. As Joaquin sat on the porch, the dog placed his front legs on the young Ranger's thighs just as he had done for years and Joaquin hugged him tightly, stroking his soft coat of unkempt hair. He sobbed, "Oh, Solo. What *am* I to do, boy?"

He felt the warmth of his old friend, smelled the familiar scent as he buried his face in the old dog's soft coat of hair, drawing the very essence of the dog's persona through his nostrils. Joaquin leaned back, holding the dog's head gently between his hands. "Whatever I decide, you'll be there for me, won't you, *mi compañero?*"

The old dog smiled, wagging his tail, leaned in close and licked the tears from Joaquin's face.

CHAPTER ELEVEN

Joaquin Campbell, standing beside his captain inside the Blue Belle Saloon in Naco, Arizona Territory, rested his sweating right hand on his revolver. The insolent face contorted with anger. Joe Hanson, better known to his friends as Slim, cussed and fumed at Captain Harry Wheeler. Joaquin turned at a right angle from Wheeler to keep an eye on the rough men inside the saloon. The bartender approached. Joaquin pointed at the man. "Back off! Tend to your own business." The man hesitated, apparently thought better of his original intention, turned, and walked back behind the bar. A man next to the bar shouted, "Damned Rangers!"

Wheeler drew the .45 from the holster at his waist and spoke with hardness to his voice. "You can go peaceable like, Hanson, or I'll bend the barrel of this revolver over your damn head and drag you over to the Ranger office." He now had the undivided attention of the proprietor of the Blue Bell Saloon.

"Now, lookee here, Wheeler. I didn't say I wouldn't talk to you." He licked his lips, his small, beady eyes shifting from the captain to the young ranger beside him. "Did I? Huh?"

Wheeler shifted his gun barrel toward the door of the saloon. "*Move.* I won't be asking you again."

"All right, all right, dammit. Put the gun up. I'll go with you."

The three men exited the saloon and walked several

blocks to the small building housing the Ranger Headquarters in Naco, Arizona. After becoming Captain of the Arizona Rangers, Harry Wheeler had moved their headquarters from Douglas, believing crime-ridden Naco needed
more attention.

As he followed Hanson inside, Wheeler hung his
flat-brimmed Stetson on a peg near the door. "Have a seat."
He motioned to the chair near his desk. The bar owner reluctantly sat down. Joaquin seated himself between Wheeler and the door. Several saddles and tack were strewn along
the walls in the office. Next to the calendar, a telephone
hung from the wall directly behind the desk. The telephone,
one of several modern conveniences in 1907, had proven an
excellent tool for lawmen at the turn of the twentieth cen-
tury. Joaquin personally liked ice cream parlors and tooth-
paste in a tube much better than telephones, but he fully
understood the significance in quick communication for
law enforcement agencies.

Joaquin studied Hanson as he sat glaring at Captain
Wheeler. The man had pinched sallow cheeks, small dark
eyes that darted all over the room. His thinning dark hair
was combed straight back on his head. As he fidgeted in his
chair, sweat stains appeared under his arms and on the neck
of his white shirt.

"Well?" Hanson rasped.

Wheeler leaned forward, his elbows resting on the
desk. He looked directly at the nefarious man in front of
him. "What do you know of Ranger Calhoun's death?"

Hanson laughed, his eyes darting quickly to Joaquin. "He's dead, ain't he?"

Wheeler reached across the desk and slapped him
hard, then back-handed him, almost knocking him from
the chair.

Hanson touched his reddened cheek. "Hey. You

can't do that to me!"

"I certainly can, Slim, and *by God*, you'll like it."

Hanson was stunned; blood trickled down his chin, fear showing in his eyes for the first time.

Wheeler sat back in his chair. "Now. Where exactly were you the night Ranger Calhoun was murdered?"

"I was ... in my saloon." He wiped at the blood on his chin, his hands trembled.

Drumming his fingers on the desk top, Wheeler chewed on his lip awhile. "That's kinda strange there, Slime."

"My name's Slim. And what do ya mean?"

"I *mean* I've talked to several patrons who were in your saloon that night. None of 'em saw *you* there."

Hanson leaned forward in his seat then sat back, brushed at his hair nervously with his hand. "I was upstairs ... with one of the girls."

"Uh huh. Which one?"

"Amelia." Joaquin shifted in his chair. Hanson's eyes darted back and forth.

Wheeler looked at Joaquin. "Why don't you go find Amelia and bring her on over here, Joaquin?"

Hanson interjected, "She ain't here no more. Gone back to Mexico, or so I heard."

Wheeler's voice was hard again, "Mighty handy for you, I'd say."

"Look! She just left. I don't know where the hell she went. They come and go all the time," shouted Hanson, his voice now shrill.

"Can anyone else confirm your alibi?" asked Wheeler.

Hanson frowned and then rubbed the back of his neck. "No. I ... I don't think so. I mean, we were together all night. Look here. I didn't kill no Ranger. There's no love lost between me and you Rangers, but I ain't lookin' for trouble by killing no Ranger. You hear me?"

Wheeler remained seated, studying the thin man. Hanson stood, shaking his finger at the captain. "Did you hear me? Dammit, I didn't kill that Ranger or have anything to do with it!"

Joaquin spoke softly, "Cap'n, may I?"

Wheeler turned toward him. "Why, sure. Go ahead."

"Please, sit down, Mr. Hanson," asked Joaquin.

"You ... go to hell!" retorted the bar owner.

Wheeler stood. "*Sit*! Or I'll sit you."

Hanson sat. Joaquin walked over, reached down and lifted first the man's right boot then his left.

Hanson shrilled, "What the hell is *this*! You can't—"

"Shut up!" thundered Wheeler. He looked at Joaquin, who shook his head. "Son, you have any further questions for this man?

Gazing directly into Hanson's eyes, Joaquin said, "You and your cronies assaulted Billy Calhoun that night, and you, you son-of-a-bitch, you fired the fatal shot at close range. *Admit it!*"

"I did nothin' of the sort! You can't pin that murder on me." Hanson's beady eyes didn't waver, solidly locked with Joaquin's blazing, brown eyes.

Wheeler intervened. "You have anything else, son?"

"No sir. I reckon not," returned Joaquin.

Scratching his head, Wheeler turned toward Hanson. "All right. You're free to go for now." Hanson hesitated. Wheeler waved his hand toward the door. "Go on! That's all for now." Hanson reached the door, opened it.

Wheeler said, "Next time I call for you, you come freely on your own. You understand me?"

The saloon proprietor turned his blazing red eyes

and hate-filled, pallid face toward the Ranger Captain. He started to say something, apparently thought better of it, and slammed the door shut behind him.

CHAPTER TWELVE
Douglas, Arizona Territory

Joaquin Campbell's head snapped back sharply, awakening him as he dozed in the wooden chair. He removed his boots from the table in the bunkhouse at Ranger headquarters. His stomach growled as he rubbed his eyes. Frank Shaw reclined on his bunk bed reading a cheap dime novel to Chapo Carter.

Shaw peered closely at a page, turning the book to get as much direct light as possible. His tongue played at the corners of his mouth. "The ... *vo*-lop ...u-us woman bent over Wild Bill. Bill's breath quickened as he looked—"

"Say, what the hell is ... *ve*-lup ... whatever the hell you jest said, Pancho?"

"Don't you be interruptin' me, Chapo. This here is the *best* part o' the whole damn book," returned Shaw impatiently.

"Wel-l-l ... all right." Carter sat up on the top bunk, swinging his legs over the side. "But, jest the same I'd like to know what the hell it means."

Shaw snorted and slapped the opened book hard against his leg. "It means ..." He hesitated, thinking hard before responding. "Well, it *means* the woman has ... uh ... big ... breaststsisus." he nodded emphatically.

"Ohhh. Uh huh." Carter pursed his lips, looking off in the distance as if pondering on the gravity of his fellow Ranger's statement.

Joaquin was fully awake, and as he listened to his

fellow Rangers, a grin formed on his face.

Shaw settled back on his pillow, placing the book once more in the most direct light for reading. "Lemme see. Where was I? Oh, yeah. 'Wild Bill's breath quickened as he looked plumb *directly* into them breaststisus, his hands gripping the soft, red satin sheets on the bed—'"

Carter sighed softly, swung his legs back up on the bed, and placed his interlaced hands beneath his head as he closed his eyes. He interrupted again. "Aw, Pancho, read to me jest *one more time* ... 'bout them ... *satan* sheets."

Joaquin chuckled as Shaw began to read the story again to the older Ranger. He strode out of the bunkhouse and into the adjacent well-lit office. Newly commissioned Captain of the Arizona Rangers, Harry Wheeler, was talking to the United States Attorney, JLB Alexander. Alexander was well dressed as usual in a clean dark suit and tie. Joaquin admired the federal prosecutor for the difficult job he always seemed to accomplish, and he truly liked him personally for being a decent human being.

"You catch 'em, Harry, and I'll deport 'em," said Alexander, laughing softly. Joaquin knew he was referring to preparations in place for deportation hearings against any apprehended Mexican revolutionaries.

"Sounds good to me, JLB. Governor Kibbey ordered me to arrest any Mexican citizens secretly gathering here in Douglas. Allegedly, there's a bunch of them meeting tonight, plotting revolutionary activities against President Porfirio Diaz's government."

"You know where, exactly?"

"I do."

"And who these men are?"

"Yessir."

Alexander pushed paper and pen across the desk to

the Captain. "Write it all down—location, names, precisely what you expect to find." He looked at the telephone hanging on the wall in the office. "I'll call the magistrate judge and write up a search warrant for him to approve." Alexander looked at Joaquin, then at Wheeler. "Gentlemen, we can't allow this sort of activity to continue unabated in the United States." He frowned. "Even if we *don't* give a damn for Diaz's method of running things in Mexico."

***

The visible half-moon barely illuminated the landscape as the partial cloud cover presented an ominous aura to the cool fall night. The column of heavily armed Rangers found their way cautiously along the narrow Douglas Street near the border with Mexico. Several dogs barked in the neighborhood, a man cursed loudly in Spanish. They halted suddenly. Captain Wheeler pointed out a darkened small adobe house directly ahead of them. Joaquin saw that all the shades had been pulled down with little light emanating from the windows and into the street.

It seemed more than two days ago when he and Wheeler had interviewed Joe Hansen, the suspect in ordering Ranger Calhoun's death and the gun running operation out of Naco. Hansen, known as Slim to his friends, ran one of the dance halls in Naco. Neither Wheeler nor Joaquin liked the nefarious man, but they could not establish that he was responsible for shooting Calhoun and knifing the prostitute. Joaquin had said nothing to Wheeler, but he felt Hansen might very well be responsible for ordering the killings and selling guns and ammunition to the Yaquis in Mexico. Joaquin had learned a great deal from watching Wheeler conduct the interview. Lessons he planned on using himself later in his law enforcement career—if indeed there was to be one.

With his left hand, Joaquin felt for his father's old Colt .45 in the belt holster. After assuring it was there, he reached for the other revolver encased in a shoulder holster under his left arm pit. *What am I checking them for again anyways?* His palms were sweaty, his heartbeat quickening. He shifted the double-barrel shotgun from his right hand to his left, careful to keep the barrel up as he looked around. The other Rangers were similarly armed: Wheeler, Carter, Shaw, and two other Rangers working out of Douglas. Another contingent of Arizona Rangers was raiding a house a half-mile or so from their position. It was time to move in, and they all knew it.

Wheeler signaled for Carter, Shaw, and Joaquin to cover the back of the house. They slipped silently around the corner of the adobe building. Carter knelt about ten yards away and directly in front of the small back door with Joaquin and Shaw taking up a position on the south side, near the door and adjacent to the adobe wall. There would be no cross-fire accidents with them shooting each other— if it came to that.

Wheeler's loud authoritative commands shattered the silence of the quiet fall evening. "Arizona Rangers! *Venga afuera! Manos arriba!* Come out! Hands up!"

Pandemonium broke loose. Men shouted, cursed. Glass and wood shattered. Something crashed through one of the windows near Joaquin and landed with a thud. He heard other Rangers slamming hard against the front door and again with sounds of the door splintering and then giving way. Men screamed. Pistol shots cracked then the loud boom of a shotgun, both barrels simultaneously. Another scream. High-pitched this time. Grunts, groans. Men struggling in mortal combat.

The back door swung open suddenly. Light spilled out into the dark desert landscape. The silhouette of a man appeared, followed closely by others all jammed together in their effort to escape. Carter's voice echoed out in the still night air. "*Alto*, you sumbitches. *No se muevan!*"

A pistol appeared in the first man's fist; he hesitated, searching out his foe in the dark, but the tide of rushing men behind him forced him on out the doorway and toward Carter. *Blam!* The loud report of the pistol and the subsequent muzzle flash pierced the darkness, reverberating off Joaquin's ear drums. Carter's shotgun answered. The man screamed horribly as he was nearly cut in half from the blast from both barrels of Carter's shotgun.

Another man ran out the door, turning toward Joaquin's position near the south wall of the house. Joaquin yelled, "*Parese!*" but the man came on. *What the heck does he have in his hand?* Joaquin instinctively ducked, feeling the wind whip above his head as the sharp machete clanged off the adobe wall. He squeezed one trigger of the shotgun. The blast caught the man fully in the face, blood and bone matter splattered the young Ranger and the wall of the house.

Joaquin heard other pistols firing; Shaw fired his shotgun while standing next to him. *God, my ear drums!* Another form materialized in the night, coming straight at him. He couldn't see a weapon, dropped to his knees, and swung the shotgun barrel low at the man's lower legs. It cracked hard against bone; the man yelped as he fell to the ground. Joaquin drew his revolver and stuck it in the man's face, his voice rasping out to his adversary, "*No se mueva.*" The man did not move. Sensing a foul odor, Joaquin realized the man had lost control of his bowels.

The raid ended quickly, the entire assault taking no more than ten minutes. Joaquin stood inside the adobe house holding a shotgun on twelve prisoners who were huddled together in a corner of the room. Their fingers

were interlaced and placed on top of their heads. Looking
to his left, he saw a large stack of wooden boxes all marked,
"Danger. Dynamite."

Wheeler tossed several flags and assorted printed
material on the floor next to the explosives. He turned to
Carter. "What the hell is *La Junta?*"

Chapo shook his head. "Don't reckon as I've heerd
o' 'em, boss."

Wheeler thought a moment. Then he picked up
several pieces of correspondence from the floor, reading
through them. "Well, I'll be damned. It's a letter from some
head honchos in Los Angeles telling these boys it's their
duty to blow up buildings in Naco and Cananea, Mexico."

"Naw ?" questioned Carter.

"I don't read Spanish real well, but that's the gist of
it." Wheeler smiled. "Hell, boys we've just stopped immi-
nent attacks on two towns south of the border." He looked
again at the letter. "And there are names and addresses of
these *La Junta* folks in Los Angeles. I'd say there'll be more
arrests in California before too long."

Joaquin spoke up, "Ole JLB, by Gawd, Alexander
will be plumb happy." He remembered Elliott's description
of the former Rough Rider, turned head prosecutor for the
Arizona Territory.

Carter laughed out loud. "Damned if he won't
at thet, son." He looked at Joaquin's pale face covered in
blood and brain matter. Taking the shotgun from him, he
placed the muzzle in the air, the butt against his pistol belt.
He put his other arm around Joaquin's shoulders, speaking
softly to him so the Mexican prisoners would not hear him,
"You all right, boy?"

Joaquin's ears were still ringing, he was bone-tired,
had a pounding headache, and he had tasted bile in his
throat several times. He pushed it all aside and smiled at

Carter. "I'm fine, Chapo. I reckon just fine." He looked down into the pale, frightened faces of the Mexicans sitting on the floor. *I'm no worse off than these poor souls, and a helluva lot better than them dead ones outside.*

CHAPTER THIRTEEN

Elliott clearly saw the man claw for his gun that was secured in the tied-down holster at his side. He waited for his own draw. *Maybe this is the son-of-a-bitch who'll kill me.* The six-shooter appeared in the killer's hand, and almost in slow motion, the muzzle came up to shooting position. *Damned tortuga! Slower'n molasses, by Gawd.* Elliott swiftly drew his own .45 Colt as the other gunman fired, flame and lead spewing out into the saloon's dark interior.

Elliott felt the hot round tug at his cotton shirt as it passed by his left side. He was already thumbing the hammer back with the heel of his left hand. Firing rapidly, he saw all three rounds hit the man squarely in the center of mass, flinging him back onto one of the tables in the saloon. The killer struggled to lift himself and bring his revolver to bear on Elliott one last time. Elliott brought his revolver up to eye level while cocking the single-action weapon quickly with his left thumb. He fired. The round entered the man's right eye, blood and bone matter exploded out the back of his head.

Elliott woke up suddenly, startled out of the horrible dream. He bolted to a sitting position in bed, sweating and gasping for air. Running his hand through his thick white hair, he felt perspiration running in rivulets down his face, chest and back. *No! My Gawd, not them nightmares again.* He swung his legs over the bed, still breathing hard and feeling dizzy, sick to his stomach. Leaning down, he rested his elbows on his thighs with his head down between his knees. Slowly, he began to feel better. Releasing air from his lungs, he sighed. *I reckon I got to pay fer my sins, Gawd. I was plumb wrong fer killin' most o' them men in my younger days, an' I'm plumb sorry fer it.*

He stood, feeling the cool of the early morning air on his moist body. Reaching down to the small bed-side table, he retrieved the old brown rosary. He knelt in front of the cross hanging on the wall beside the bed, and closed his eyes. The familiar worn wooden beads aided him in his prayers to his God. *Glory be to the father, the son, and the holy ghost ...*

***

Megan Elliott awoke. It was dark in the bedroom, still too early to rise for the day's work. She felt for her husband, and not finding him in bed, sat upright, searching in the darkened room. At last she saw him slumped over, kneeling below the cross. *The nightmares again.* She wanted to go to him, hold him, console him somehow, but she knew better. Lying back onto her pillow, she waited until he had finished praying. As he stood, she called affectionately out to him, "Samuel T. Come here ol' man."

Elliott hesitated. Then he walked to the bed and slipped under the covers beside his wife. "I'm plumb sorry, Meg, if I woke you too early." As she moved next to him, he wrapped his arms around her. She rested her head on his chest and waited awhile before answering. "Are you all right?"

The strong man sighed heavily and did not answer right away. Megan waited silently. Snippets of light began to enter the room.

He said, "It's them nightmares. I reckon they've been worse lately fer some reason or 'nother."

"Why do you suppose they're coming more frequently?"

Sighing again, Elliott said, "I jest—" He swallowed hard. "I jest *don't* know, Meg."

Kissing her gently on the forehead, he continued, "It's all right. Don't you worry none 'bout me." His furrowed brow told her different.

"Is there something I should know?"

He hesitated, chewing on the inside of his cheek. "Yes, Megan. I reckon there is."

She waited for him to continue.

"A man come by the ranch sometime ago. When you was workin' on the garden o'er on Cienega Crick."

Megan held her tongue, knowing he was far from done talking. His blue eyes looked into her hazel eyes. "He's a badun', Meg." Elliott's jaw was set hard when he continued, "He's a damn killer, I'd say."

Megan sat up in bed, her face now showing fright. "Why would he come here?" Elliott did not respond. "Why *here?*" she queried more urgently.

"His boss knew me from years ago when I hired my gun out." He frowned again. They want me to help 'em fight the Rangers. I reckon Wheeler and his men have been trouble fer 'em in their dealings along the border."

Her eyes widened. "And if you *don't* help them?"

Elliott didn't respond. Megan gripped his arm tightly. "What are these people capable of?"

Still he said nothing.

"Would they harm you ... us?" She repeated the unanswered question. "Would they *harm* us? Her voice was elevated.

"I won't let thet happen, Meg. You ought to know thet."

She was silent for a moment. "I'm sorry, Elliott. You've *always* been there for me and Timmy."

He smiled. "No need to be sorry."

She snuggled closer to the man she deeply loved. "And I'll always be here for you. Always."

"I reckon I *know* thet, lil' missy," he retorted.

Megan smiled. She was already looking forward to spending another good day with the man she loved. *Thank you, God. And please don't be so hard on him. He's such a good man.* But then she knew He had to know all about Samuel T. Elliott.

CHAPTER FOURTEEN

The night was deathly quiet as a full moon lit up the desert landscape and the ranch house. The mountain range several miles to the south in Mexico stood out against the darkened sky twinkling with stars. A coyote howled, followed within minutes by several coyotes answering the challenge. One of the horses in the corral snorted, ears perked up suddenly while two dark shadows moved stealthily from the barn toward the ranch house.

"I don't want no part of it, Gonzo," whispered the smaller man as he hesitated in his stride. The larger man in the lead, turned quickly, slapping the other across the face. "*Cobarde*," he hissed. "You weel do thees or I weel keel you, *culero.*"

The smaller man's frightened face gazed at the hate-filled, dark face glowering at him in the moonlight night. Sweating profusely, he swallowed hard. "All right, *dammit!* I'll help. Just keep your filthy hands off me."

The Mexican man grinned, showing a gap in his front teeth. His dark unshaven face glistened in the moonlight; the ugly scar along the right side of his face accentuated his disposition. He was a large man with powerful arms and a thick set, heavy body. He held a piece of iron in his left hand that he shifted back over to his right hand. A large skinning knife was encased in a leather sheath on his belt. "*No me jodas. Comprende?*

"I *said* I would do it, didn't I?" rasped the small man.

Turning abruptly, Gonzalez proceeded toward the

ranch house with the smaller man in tow. Reaching the front door, he motioned for the smaller man to hold the sagging screen door open. He slowly opened the wooden door, cringing as it creaked on its rusty hinges. Both men slipped quietly inside and moved to the only adjacent room which served as a bedroom for rancher Sam Plunkett and an elderly friend Ed Kennedy. The men slept in beds situated in two corners of the small room. Plunkett snored loudly; Kennedy restlessly turned on his side.

Gonzalez surveyed the room, spying a gold pocket watch lying on a small table next to Plunkett. His eyes glistened brightly in the moonlight as he gazed at the watch. Cautiously he crept forward, the iron piece clutched tightly in his fist. Almost within reach of the sleeping rancher, he stopped, and motioned impatiently for his partner behind him to approach the other bed.

Hesitantly, the smaller man complied.

Satisfied with his accomplice's actions, Gonzalez now stood over the sleeping rancher. Raising the iron piece over his head, he whispered, "*Quien es el jefe, ahora?* Huh, cabron?" Spittle spewed from his mouth as he struck hard. The heavy weapon fashioned from a wagon tongue struck Plunkett's skull, easily crushing it. Gonzalez struck again, and again while saying, "Who's the boss, now?"

The smaller assailant was struggling with the elderly man. The old man yelled out, "What the *hell* is goin' on, Ascencion? Get off me, damn you!"

Gonzalez strode quickly to where they were struggling. He swung the bloodied weapon in a high arc, up and down with all the strength in his massive arms. Kennedy's skull gave way to the force of the blow, and he sagged against Ascension. Gonzalez dropped the heavy weapon and drew his knife. "Hold heem up, damn you!" And as his accomplice did so, he drove the knife into Kennedy's chest again and again, blood pouring over his hands and his clothes. The old man's body slumped over, but Gonzalez continued stabbing and slashing.

"*Basta! Enough!*" screamed Ascension. He released his hold on the elderly man.

The bloodied, crazed Gonzalez grabbed his accomplice by the shirt front, dragging him across the room to the other bed where rancher Sam Plunkett lay bludgeoned to death. Gonzalez extended the knife to Ascension. "Take eet. And finish heem," he said hoarsely.

The smaller man backed away his eyes wide with fright. He shook his head, "No. *No!*"

A smile curled at Gonzalez's lips. "Then *you* watch, *culero*. And see how a *man* keels." He knelt quickly and stabbed the bludgeoned rancher repeatedly, then slashed his throat. Blood flowed everywhere. Ascencion watched in horror, then he turned and vomited on the floor.

CHAPTER FIFTEEN
Village of Sonoita, Arizona Territory, 1907

C armen Campbell sat next to Hao Li cradling the baby in her arms as Li the buckboard pulled up next to the board sidewalk in front of the store. The painted wooden sign out front displayed a simple message to all who ventured by, "Clem's Mercantile." The Chinaman didn't normally travel to town for supplies or any other reason, but now that she had the baby to care for, she asked him for his help. He had not hesitated in agreeing, but she knew from his look he hadn't wanted to go into town where most folks looked down on the Chinese.

Carmen stepped down from the buckboard with Hao Li's assistance. Suddenly without warning, one of the new "horseless carriages" drove past. The driver honked the horn. The startled team of horses tried to rear, couldn't do so, and panicked. Hao Li sprang forward and settled them down.

Damn those contraptions! Seething with anger, Carmen watched as the noisy machine continued down the main street; the driver clothed in a long duster with cap and goggles. *I agree with Elliott. They ought to outlaw those things.*

Hao Li held the door for her as she entered the store to the jingle of an attached bell as the door swung closed behind them. The interior of Clem's Mercantile included a spacious room cluttered with everything in the way of goods anyone could ever hope to want in life. Buying the items was a hoss of a different color as Elliott would say. The old wood floor creaked as Carmen walked toward the counter where the cash register was located. Numerous glass candy jars adorned the counter top with the shelves behind stocked full of an assortment of canned goods, sacks of flour, sugar, and other staples. She couldn't help but glance admiringly at the brand-new clothes stacked neatly on shelves to her right—pretty dresses and hats for the ladies, work clothes, boots and hats for men. A U.S. Post Office station was located in the rear of the store.

The proprietor Clem stood behind the counter. Carmen had never liked the man, but his store was the closest for necessary shopping. She knew for years without anyone telling her that he did not like having Mexicans in his store. However, he was no fool and did not seem to mind taking their money along with the gringos'. Clem frowned as Carmen approached him. He was dressed in a clean white shirt with a black bow tie, his sparse, gray hair was combed back, and a small mustache was neatly trimmed on his cleanly shaven face. Two men stood across the counter from him; apparently they had been talking.

He acknowledged her presence, and said curtly, "Carmen. What brings you here today?"

Carmen looked him squarely in the eyes before speaking. His eyes wavered, and he looked down, stammering, "*Well?*"

Placing a list of supplies on the counter, she said, "We need supplies for the ranch, Clem." She re-adjusted her hold on the baby, looking directly at him, her face grim.

He fumbled with the list, glancing sideways at the two men standing across from him. Annoyed, she looked at both men. One wore a derby hat perched high on his head. His round ruddy face was sporting a large red mustache. Wearing store-bought clothes and polished dress shoes, he insolently looked her up and down, taking his time as he appraised her.

Derby Hat spoke, "Well now, Clem—I wasn't aware you let chinks *an'* greasers in your store." He grinned broadly. "Even if the Messicans are lil' pretty ones." He continued to stare at her, a smirk on his face.

Clem cleared his throat, looking away from Carmen. "I don't like either of 'em coming in here." Clearing his throat again, his eyes averted. "It's bad for business." He looked over at Carmen then at the floor again. "I've told you before; just because you're married to a white don't make *you* one."

Carmen's face reddened, her eyes narrowed. "I'm not interested in your opinion, Clem, or being white. I guess my money spends the same as any other." She felt Hao Li move quietly beside her and the baby.

The second man spoke sharply, "Who's the chink?"

Carmen turned toward him, and looking into his eyes, she had a bad feeling in the pit of her stomach. She gasped, taking a step back. He was dressed in black and his black hat band was adorned with small silver conchos. But his eyes—they were small, green, and piercing. She saw raw meanness in the man, a ruthless, dangerous look. Then she saw the pearl-handled six-guns he wore, low on his hips. Her stomach tightened again. *We must get out of here. Now!*

She turned, clutching her baby tightly, saying, "Never mind, Clem; another day perhaps. Come on Li, let's go home."

A hard, cruel voice stopped her dead in her tracks. "Not so fast! You'll not leave till *I* say you damn well can." Derby Hat snickered.

"Let 'em go, Slydell. They ain't hurtin' nobody," stammered Clem.

"Shut up, damn you!" shouted the gunman. He stepped toward them. Hao Li moved quickly to stand in front of Carmen and the baby.

"No trouble plees," the Chinaman said.

Derby Hat spoke. "Move aside, Slydell. I'll show this chink son-of-a-bitch some real manners around whites."

He moved past the gunman, swinging hard with his right fist. Hao Li spun his left arm out away from his body, easily blocking the haymaker punch with his forearm. Simultaneously, he punched straight out with his right, palm open, the heel of his hand catching Derby Hat fully on the chin then onto his mouth, nose, and eyes. The man's head snapped back, the derby hat flying off. The Chinaman stepped in close, turning right as his edged left hand moved in close to his own body then snapped out sharply, striking the man fully in the throat.

Carmen heard the force of the blow, a sickening thud. *No. No! I don't want this.* She pulled her baby boy closer as she screamed, "No, Li!"

Derby Hat teetered, holding his throat. His eyes wide, mouth open, but he could not speak or breathe. He made a strange sound, guttural animal groan. Hao Li kicked him sharply in the groin. Derby Hat jerked forward, trying to hold both his throat and groin. As his head dropped, the Chinaman brought his knee up into Derby Hat's face; a hard, smashing blow that knocked the man back and onto to the floor. He lay there; his eyes rolled back in his head and he did not move again.

Hao Li turned swiftly toward the gunman, who was momentarily stunned by the quickness of the Chinaman's actions. The killer recovered quickly and like lightning, his deadly six-gun appeared from nowhere. But the old Chinaman was a fraction faster, kicking hard to his left with his right leg. The .45 Colt jarred loose from the gunman's hand. It spun in the air, crashing into canned goods on the top shelf behind the counter. The cans moved ever so slightly, then all the contents from the shelf collapsed, cans spilling out onto the floor and on top of Clem. Several cans struck his head with glancing blows.

Clem staggered and screamed, "I'm hit!" He felt his head and then looked at bloody hand. He screamed again, his eyes wide with fright. "Oh, my God, I'm bad hurt."

Hao Li did not wait for the gunman to react to losing his six-shooter; he gathered himself quickly and struck at the man in black. Balancing on his left foot, he extended his right leg and foot, kicking the man directly in the chest with all the strength he could muster. The force of the kick slammed the gunman back into shelves containing clothing and other mercantile. The shelves gave way; items scattered across the room.

Hatless and somewhat shaken, the gunman staggered to his feet, his small green eyes sharp, pointed like daggers. Gasping, holding his chest with his left hand, he reached down into his left boot and swiftly withdrew a small derringer pistol. As he cocked the hammer, he rasped, "By God, I'll *kill* you for this. You ... you goddamned yella bastard!" He raised the derringer. Carmen screamed, "No!"

A loud, deep voice boomed out into the room, "Hold it!" The gunman hesitated, frowned, and leaned forward again with the pistol.

"I said, "*No!* Damn you, Slydell. You work for *me*, and you'll do as you're told."

The gunman dropped his arm and cursed loudly. Carmen turned toward the entrance to the store and saw a large, heavy-set man standing just inside the room. His hands were on his hips as he surveyed the room and what had transpired. He wore an expensive felt hat and equally expensive suit and tie with meticulously polished boots. She thought he must have cut a handsome figure in his day, but now in middle age, he was sporting a large belly and his red face betrayed alcohol abuse over the years. But he still commanded a room with his loud, booming voice, and he resonated with power and strength.

He strode forward and stepped in close to Carmen, looking first at her, then the baby she clutched tightly to her breast. Quickly, he peered at the gunman, saying in a softer voice, "Easy now, Slydell. You just calm down. I'll handle this *my* way."

The gunman pleaded, "Let me kill 'em, Mr. Hyde. Goddamn him to hell!"

Hyde's gaze went to Hao Li; he motioned curtly for him to leave the store. "Go on ... *Git*! ... git on outta here. *Now*! Before Slydell here kills ya."

The old Chinaman looked at Carmen. She said, "Let's go out to the buckboard, Li."

"I'll kill ya, ya yella *bastard*!" screamed the gunman. "One of these days—"

Hao Li turned, moving quickly toward the door, Carmen right behind him. Hyde said, "Not you, miss. Not just yet. I'm not finished with you."

Carmen hesitated, handed the baby to Li, and as he hurried out the door, she turned toward the man who had saved them from certain death. "I thank you, Mister—?"

The voice boomed out. "Hyde's the name. Ben Hyde."

She sighed, releasing air from her lungs. "Thank you, Mister Hyde."

The man seemed even larger up close, barrel-chested with a thick, short neck. He looked at her as he pulled a cigar from his pocket and lit it with a match. He puffed on the cigar.

Carmen took a step back. *What's he up to? I don't like him either. Not one darn bit.*

Finally, he spoke. "You're that Messican girl that married the Ranger ... what's his name?"

"*Si Senor*. My husband is Joaquin Campbell."

"Yeah." He hesitated again while he puffed on the cigar. "Your husband. I understand he's real close to an old friend of mine—Elliott. You know him?"

"Yes sir. I've known Elliott all my life. He's been a good friend to my family for years."

Hyde placed his cigar between his teeth and took off his jacket. Then he proceeded to roll up his long shirt sleeves. "Damn. It's hot in here." He swung his jacket over his right shoulder, tipped his hat back on his head, and placed his left hand in his pocket. It was then she noticed a strange tattoo on his right forearm. Several emblems of some sort?

Hyde took the cigar from his teeth. "You go on home and take that chink son-of-a-bitch with you. Next time my man Slydell sees him, he'll kill 'em for sure, and I won't interfere." Hyde pointed a finger at her. "We don't cotton to his kind around here. You understand me?" His face reddened. Carmen stepped back.

Quickly Hyde smiled, stepped closer, and patted her on the shoulder. "Now you be sure and tell your friend Elliott I helped you out today. You tell him *Ben Hyde* helped."

"Yes sir, I surely will," she said.

"Good girl. You tell him I did him a good turn. Now he owes *me*. You tell him I'm still waitin' for him to come work for me." His eyes were hard, for just a moment. "Now, I'm a patient man, but I ain't waitin' much longer for his answer." He waved her toward the door. "Go on now. Git along home."

As Carmen moved swiftly out of the store to the buckboard, she heard the gunman cursing loudly and arguing with Ben Hyde. She bounded up into the seat, taking the baby from the Chinaman. Hao Li got the horses moving quickly.

Carmen looked over at her friend and patted his hand. "It's not your fault, Li." He did not respond. She saw the worried look on his tense face, his jaw set, eyes glaring, focused on the road ahead. Carmen closed her eyes and suppressed a sob. *Why are people so ugly and mean?*

CHAPTER SIXTEEN

An early evening breeze stirred the dusty street of Sonoita. Joaquin closed his eyes briefly. As he turned his face to avoid the dust kicked up from a small gust of hot summer air. Tired of waiting in the narrow alley, he seethed with anger. *Come on, you sumbitch!* He gazed at the storefront, his jaw set hard. He knew his boss, Captain Wheeler, would not approve of him being here, but there were certain things in life you just did not allow to occur again. No, his purpose was clear to him; he knew damned well what must be done tonight.

The sun set. A bright orange glow accentuated the impending evening sky. Dusk approached, then was gone as well, the darkness filling the void of a long day for the young Ranger. The light inside the store was extinguished. Several moments passed; the front door to the store opened, bell jingling. A woman stumbled out, followed by a man dressed in a suit and tie.

"Go on, *git* !" He kicked her hard in the buttocks after stepping out onto the board sidewalk. She fell headlong into the street. Pulling the door to, he bent to secure the lock with the key in his hand. "I'm finished with you. Messican *puta*."

Joaquin stepped quickly out of the dark alley and strode forward. He reached into the front pocket of his pants, found the folded pocket knife, and secured it in his right fist.

The man straightened as he withdrew the key from

the lock. He turned toward the street, a frown forming on a white, pallid face. Joaquin saw the neatly trimmed mustache, the black hair slicked back on his head.

"What the—?" the man stammered.

Stepping onto the board sidewalk past the prostrate woman, Joaquin hit him square in the face with his right fist that clutched the folded pocket knife. The force of the punch snapped the man's head back and the rest of him followed as he smashed into the secured glass door. Blood poured from the broken nose he held with both hands. Raw fear exuded from a face bloodied and wide-eyed.

Joaquin stepped in close and hooked a hard blow to the man's mid-section with his right, then a quick left hook to his jaw, knocking him to the board side walk.

"Clem. You *son-of-a-bitch!*" he rasped. "You ever treat my wife and my friend Li like you did the other day, I'll beat you within an inch of your miserable life."

Clem scooted back several feet on the sidewalk away from the man standing over him. Wide-eyed, he attempted to focus on who was speaking to him. He spat a tooth and blood out on the dusty sidewalk. "Young Campbell ... that you?"

Breathing heavily, Joaquin said nothing, his jaw clenched, glaring at the downed man.

"I ... I meant ... no disrespect." Clem swallowed blood, choked on it, spat again. "Please don't hurt me." His hands were up in front of his face.

"You damn well meant it, you pompous ass. *Stand up!*"

Placing his clasped pocket knife in his pocket, Joaquin grasped the struggling man by his jacket, hauled him up from the sidewalk, and slammed him against the door. Through clenched teeth, he said, "You'll get no more business from our ranch." Clem began to slump to the sidewalk. "I said to *stand*, you miserable wretch."

"I'll ... I'll report you to the law."

Joaquin slapped both his ears hard then smashed Clem's head back into the glass door; more glass broke. Clem screamed.

"I *am* the law, you arrogant bastard. You press charges against me, and I'll arrest you for assault and battery on that woman lying in the street."

The man groaned. "Oh, my God. You've hurt me bad."

"*Shut up.* Who was the gunman in your store the other day?"

"Look, mister." The man swallowed hard, choking again, "I can't—"

Joaquin slapped him hard across the face.

"Okay. *Okay.* His name is Coburn—Slydell Coburn." Clem sobbed. "Don't hurt me anymore. Please, mister."

"You mention this to anyone, I'll come back and finish it. You understand me?"

"Yes. *Yes!*" The man cowered against the battered door.

The woman scrambled to her feet. Joaquin turned toward her.

"You all right, uh?" Joaquin asked.

She nodded and replied, "*Sí, Señor.*"

Joaquin stepped in close and studied her bruised face. "You're a fool for hanging out with the likes of him." Turning, he strode toward the paint horse tied to the hitch rack across from the store front. He vaulted into the saddle, and spurred the cow pony into a lope down the darkened, narrow street.

A half-full moon attempted to illuminate the bloodied, sobbing man who sat hunkered down on the dirty board sidewalk. The woman stood in the dusty street, unable to make a decision. Dark shadows along the street front took over and the man disappeared from view. The frightened sobbing continued intermittently. A lonely coyote howled suddenly in the quiet night.

CHAPTER SEVENTEEN

Elliott patted Viento's neck affectionately after tying him to the hitch rack in front of the barn. *You ol' rascal, we've been through a lot together, now ain't we?* Hearing a girl laugh, he turned quickly toward the house with a smile on his face. Timmy Campbell and his friend Kelly from school were sitting on the bottom steps of the porch. Kelly had just attempted to rope the steer horns attached to an old sawhorse out in front. *Darned if she didn't git one 'o them horns after all.*

Kelly flipped the rope up and off the horn, and began to coil the rope. Timmy said something to her, and she laughed. The girl's parents were inside with Megan.

Elliott reached down, picking up Viento's front hoof. He noted the badly worn toe of the horseshoe. He bent forward, his knees together, and placed the horse's leg between his legs, the bottom of the hoof facing him. Quickly, he unclenched the nails then pulled the worn shoe off, tossing it to the side.

He was glad they had invited Kelly's family over for Sunday dinner. They seemed like real nice folks even if they were citified. And the girl, Kelly. Well, she was a mighty fine human being. Of that, Elliott was sure. She brought a big smile to everyone's face, especially to Timmy. That was all that mattered to Elliott.

As Elliott stood near Viento's shoulder, he saw Timmy throw a perfect loop over both horns, then quickly pull up the slack in the rope. *Good boy!* He was sure the boy had not told Kelly he practiced hard for a full week prior to her coming out to the ranch. Smiling, he thought, *hell, I wouldn't neither, come to think of it.* Reaching down, he picked up the horse's hoof again, repositioned himself and quickly trimmed the excess growth of hoof with sharpened nippers. As he pulled a rasp from his back pocket to level the bottom of the hoof for the new shoe, his peripheral vision caught a horseman riding in from the tree line.

Squinting, he quickly scanned the horse and rider. *Damn. I can't see like I used to.* As they came closer, he saw it was Captain Harry Wheeler of the Arizona Rangers.

"*Buenas tardes, viejo.*" Wheeler smiled as he leaned forward in the saddle.

"The same to you," responded Elliott testily.

Wheeler swung down from his horse, a tall, lanky bay. "Easy hoss," he said easily. "I meant no harm."

The two men shook hands. Elliott grinned. "That's *viejito* to you. How's the rangerin' business?"

Wheeler frowned. "A couple of new folks in the Territorial Legislature submitted bills to abolish the Rangers."

"Hell. No!" Elliott spat at the ground. "Them Democrats, I'd say."

"Yeah, you're right about that. But neither bill passed. We're in the clear—at least for awhile." Wheeler's face darkened.

What brings you way out here, *jefe?*"

The Ranger Captain removed his hat and slapped it against his leg; an immediate dust cloud formed. Elliott probed, "Megan's Sunday cookin' maybe?"

It was Wheeler's turn to grin. "Well, now that you mention it." Then his disposition turned serious, his eye brows wrinkling into deep furrows. "Have you heard about Plunkett and Kennedy?"

Elliott straightened, dropping the horse's hoof and

heavy rasp to the ground. "No, I reckon not, Harry. We don't get much in the way o' news out this away."

"They were murdered. Appears like maybe while they slept."

"*What? What on earth for?* They was just a couple o' ol' men."

Wheeler tied his horse next to Viento at the hitch rack. "There's $100 cash, a gold watch, a revolver—and Gonzalez and Ascencion—all missing."

"Who the hell are they?" retorted Elliott.

"Mexican ranch employees."

Elliott grunted.

"I need your help in tracking these two men, Elliott."

Elliott shook his head, looking hard at Wheeler. "I reckon not. I'm gittin' too damn old fer law work, Harry."

Wheeler sighed, the air escaping slowly from his lungs. "I wouldn't ask if I didn't truly need the help." He pursed his lips. "As for the old part, I've got Rangers on the payroll half your age that don't hold a candle to you, and you damn well know it."

Elliott hesitated, thinking for several minutes. "You reckon they've gone to *Mexico?*" Without waiting for an answer, he said, "I recollect Sam's place ain't fer from the border."

"I believe that to be the case. It most likely will be a long, hard journey to catch them. Word is they've gone to one of the mining camps down in Sonora."

"What Rangers are goin'?"

"Joaquin Campbell and a couple of new recruits— Dick Hickey and Gene Shute."

"I'd need Chapo Carter."

"Carter's up in the Chiricahuas chasing rustlers. Don't know when I'll hear from him again," returned

Wheeler.

Elliott stroked his chin thoughtfully. He could sure use the money for several improvements he had planned for the ranch. Megan would raise billy hell with him, but maybe not so much with Joaquin going as well. "I'll want sergeant's pay."

"Done."

Elliott turned, leaning on Viento with his arms draped over the horse's back. He looked hard at the ground. Wheeler let him take his time.

Elliott said, "I reckon I kin go tomorrow."

"Excellent! You want the others to meet you at Plunkett's ranch?" asked Wheeler.

"Yep—with bells on and rarin' to go, by Gawd." He stepped around the horse close to the Ranger Captain. "You'll have supper with us, Harry?"

"Why, thank you. I'd like that."

"*Bueno.*" Elliott swung back to the gray dun, stroking his neck. "Just don't go an' mention this hyar *de*tail to Meg." He bit his lip, frowning. "Don't you spoil her Sunday, ya heah?"

Wheeler said, "She'll figure something's up. I don't come calling very often."

"Guessin' and knowin' are hosses o' a diffrent color," replied Elliott evenly.

He pulled tobacco and papers from his shirt pocket, built a smoke, lit it, and drew deeply on the cigarette. "After all the company's gone, *I'll* tell her." He sighed. *I reckon there's no point in gittin' in the dog house too soon. Might jest as well make the most o' the rest o' a good day.* He drew deeply on the cigarette again, and engrossed in thought, he forgot to exhale. Smoke seeped out his nose, hesitantly drifting away in the early evening breeze.

Elliott let out a deep breath. He looked over at

Wheeler as they walked toward the house. "You give any more thought to thet blood sign Billy Calhoun left under the rug afore he died?"

"Hansen sure appeared guilty when we interviewed him."

Elliott grinned. "Hell, he's guilty all right ... o' somethin'. But I wonder—"

"What?" Captain Wheeler stopped in his tracks.

"It seems to me it jest might be important if Billy used one finger at a time to leave sign or ... maybe he used all three fingers at once?"

"What difference would using all three fingers make?"

Elliott's eyebrows arched upward. "Don't reckon I know fer shore, but if he *did* use all three fingers when he tried to send us a message, you're lookin' at all them letters bein' the same—whatever they might be." Elliot finished his cigarette in silence; he tossed the butt down and ground it into the sandy soil with his dusty boot. "If thet's so, your boy Slim is off the hook."

"I dunno. What did Joaquin think about your theory?" asked Wheeler.

"He said it was hard to say about them letters. He couldn't recollect." Elliott turned toward the house and saw Megan waving to them from the porch. He waved back and said, "The boy'll figger it all out, Harry. Let's ease on up to the house and see if Meg has some vittles fer us, uh?"

CHAPTER EIGHTEEN
Sonora, Mexico, late summer 1907

Joaquin Campbell gingerly lifted the heavy cast iron dutch oven lid, careful to not dump any of the remaining hot coals and ashes inside the oven. The beginnings of a grin formed on his boyish face as he peered down at the freshly baked biscuits, lightly browned on top. *Hot damn! Good lookin' and the aroma—wel-l-l now.* Something nudged his leg. He looked down at the dog as he set the lid on a rock near the campfire. Solo Vino wagged his tail. "Not now, boy. Can't you see I've been charged with a very important duty? Hell, men've been shot for cookin' poorly out on the trail."

The old dog peered up at him.

"No. No, you're not gettin' any of these biscuits, even if you *are* on your best behavior." Joaquin walked over to one of the gunny sacks containing oats for the horses and mules. He reached deep down inside the sack, smiling as he felt the wooden box. Gently withdrawing the box, he set it on the ground and opened it, taking out several eggs. At least they would have a decent breakfast today.

They all met at Plunkett's ranch house several days ago—him, Elliott, and the two new recruits, Hickey and Shute. He was appalled at the carnage left behind by the killers—dried, splattered blood everywhere inside the house—on the floors, the walls, the furniture. They had removed and buried the bodies. It was obvious a heinous crime had been committed and justice needed to be served to those responsible.

The December weather remained stable with no rain thus far to obliterate the trail. One of the fugitives' horses had a rear shoe missing. Grunting, Elliott had pointed at the track, "Lookee there, *mijo*, even a blind hog gits an acorn now an' agin."

The Rangers rode hard the first day, trying to make up for lost time and to shorten the distance between them and the two killers. An informant advised Captain Wheeler the killers planned to work at several of the mines now operating in Sonora. Their horse tracks led directly to the town of Magdalena. The four heavily armed Rangers with two pack mules in tow had trotted down the dusty street of Magdalena, in the state of Sonora, Mexico.

Upon arriving, Elliott asked Colonel Kosterlitzky of the Rurales for assistance in finding the two murderers, but Kosterlitzky could not accommodate them. The Yaqui Indians were in the midst of yet another uprising against the Mexican government. Mexican President Porfirio Diaz depended heavily on his chosen Rurales in crushing the revolution as quickly as possible; they worked directly for him, and answered to no one else. Kosterlitzky had wished the Rangers well, advising them to be on the lookout for the murderous Yaqui tribesmen.

One of the new recruits approached Joaquin as he cooked scrambled eggs in the dutch oven over the campfire. Occasional smoke drifted up and away from the red-hot coals. Ranger Dick Hickey tilted his hat back on his head as he spat tobacco juice. "Hey Joaquin, what's the final tally on the *re*-ward for Gonzalez and Ascencion?"

Joaquin didn't answer. He harbored the suspicion that Hickey had joined the Rangers only for the reward offered and not from any sense of duty to bring criminals to justice. Quiet, he stirred the scrambled eggs in the hot cast iron oven.

Another voice broke the uncomfortable silence of the still morning. "Hell, Dick. I done told ya it was over $1,000 dollars ... $1,050 for the both of 'em." Gene Shute walked up to the campfire carrying canvas feed bags in either hand.

Joaquin felt Hickey watching as he set the dutch oven with the cooked eggs off to the side of the campfire. Joaquin stood, looking squarely at Hickey. "You boys help yourselves to the eggs and biscuits. Coffee's ready, next to the fire." Hickey seemed about to say something, lowered his eyes while reaching for a tin plate, and said nothing.

Elliott had advised Joaquin the other Ranger recruit Gene Shute was distantly related to the slain rancher, Plunkett, and might have joined only to avenge the killing. Reaching for his coffee cup, Joaquin stepped back from the fire. As he looked out over the horizon, the gray dawn gave way to blue skies, and a brilliant, orange sunrise cast its magic spell over the Sonoran desert. Large saguaro cacti dotted the landscape along with greasewood, mesquite, palo verde, ocotillo, and catclaw providing shade and cover for animal and man alike.

Hearing a horse approaching the camp, Joaquin quickly stepped behind a large mesquite tree next to the campfire, his hand on the butt of the Colt .45 revolver holstered at his side. Horse and rider came into view, Elliott astride the gray bay or *grulla* gelding. The old Ranger rode up and dismounted, leaving the horse ground-tied. He stood next to the horse, flipped the tapadero stirrup over the saddle, and began loosening the cinch.

"Got any coffee, *mi'jo?*" He turned, the dark weather-beaten face wrinkling in the sunlight as he grinned at Joaquin. Tipping his battered, gray Stetson back on his head with his right thumb, his left hand reached for the tobacco and papers in his front shirt pocket. Elliott's white forehead appeared in stark contrast to his brown face and neck. He built the cigarette and lit it.

Joaquin pulled the collar of his wool jacket up around his neck as he walked back to the campfire and brought Elliott a steaming hot cup of coffee. It had been cold during the previous night with an incessant cold rain. Joaquin thought, *that's the way it is in the desert, hotter'n hell during the day and colder'n all get out at night.*

Elliott gestured at Hickey and Shute who were eating out of their tin plates near the fire. "Come on o'er here, boys. I've got somethin' to say." Inhaling deeply on the cigarette as the two drew near, he said, "We're headed down to Santa Ana. There's a mining camp nearby where Gonzalez and Ascencion might be holed up." He rubbed his unshaven jaw; a frown formed on his dark face. "With the rain last night, I plumb lost their trail this mornin', but it makes sense thet's the direction they're headed."

Joaquin attempted to lighten the conversation. "The informant did say they had planned to work at several of the mines down here."

"Let's give it a try, Elliott. Hell, too much money riding on this not to keep at it," replied Hickey.

Shute grunted. "They need to be caught—hung for what they done, by God."

It was Elliott's turn to grunt. "I reckon from here on there'll be no more campfires. We'll be in the thick of Yaqui country. We run into a large war party, we're as good as dead."

Hickey asked, "Why are the Yaquis so hell-fired up against the Messicans anyways?

Elliott gulped hot coffee before answering. "It goes back several years, I reckon. When the Apaches was purty much done in by us and the Mexican government by the late 1890s, it allowed the government to put their soldiers onto the Yaqui problem. Them Mexican speculators and developers come lookin' to take a piece o' all the rich river lands the Yaquis held—had held for centuries so I've been told."

Joaquin replied, "If the land belongs to the Yaquis, why all the fighting?

Elliott forced a hard laugh. "The Mexican government figgers them Injuns never *did* have no *o*-fficial title to the land. They consider all the river lands the property of the nation. Hell, they sent in survey crews an' sech. It warn't long afore blood was spilled. Them Injuns figgered the water, meadows, and woodlands belonged to them. An' them *Mexicanos*, they was eye-balling them fertile river lands seein' they was about right fer growin' wheat, sugar, cotton, an' other crops."

Joaquin shook his head in disgust.

Shute leaned forward, now interested in the conversation. "Well, what happened?"

Elliott built another cigarette, struck a match along his pant leg, and lit it, drawing deeply on the cigarette. His eyebrows rose; he looked at Joaquin, Shute, then Hickey. "You boys shore you're interested in all this hyar *informacion?*"

In unison, they all hollered, *"Yes!"*

Smiling, he continued. "Wellsir, 'ol Cajame and Tatabiate—they was Yaqui chiefs in 1887—the first to rise up in revolt agin the Mexicans an' what they was a tryin' to do. I heerd a 1,000 warriors fought 5,000 Mexican troops to a stand still. Them Injuns done right well early on holdin' off the Mexican cavalry." He drew deeply on his cigarette. "Tit fer tat, I'd say."

"Then what happened? They're still fighting, aren't they?" Joaquin returned.

"Yep. They shore are, but it ain't jest the Mexican cavalry no more. Them Mexicans have laid railroad tracks into the sierra here. I reckon they're haulin' artillery in fer the fight an' them new ... machine guns." Elliott rubbed his unshaven chin. "Soon, it won't be no match-up fer them Injuns. They'll be crushed." His eyes hardened. "I reckon when it's all said an' done, the Mexicans'll kill 'em or sell them Injuns off as slaves fer the *blanco* planters."

Silence ensued, each man thinking of what Elliott had said.

Elliott tossed his cigarette to the ground, grinding the butt into the soil with his boot. "I wouldn't feel too badly 'bout them Injuns, if I was you, boys. It ain't our fight. Besides, them Injuns ketch us out here, they'll torture or kill us fer shore."

He tossed his empty tin cup at Joaquin, walked over to his horse Viento, and tightened the cinch on his weathered saddle. Turning, he pulled a gold watch from his pocket and gazed at it with a smile on his face. His eyes twinkled. "Accordin' to my brand-spankin' new, handy dandy watch, it's high time to git movin' fer Santa Ana. Maybe we'll find us a couple o' no good, *low down* murderers."

***

Joaquin rode silently, meandering slowly through the riparian terrain, as he followed Viento's tracks. The outer fringes of the river bottom were filled with catclaw and greasewood, and mesquite trees had begun to encroach. Along the riverbank cottonwood, velvet ash, and black willow trees billowed in the afternoon breeze; green grasses and sedges stood out in stark contrast to the shrub land as a gray hawk circled above looking for easy prey.

He pulled the two pack mules behind him with the lead rope dallied around his saddle horn. They had crossed the *Rio Yaqui* about ten miles north of La Dura searching for the two murderers at the mining camp near Santa Ana to no avail. They verified the men had been there, but left before the Rangers' arrival. All the Mexicans they contacted were deathly afraid of the warring Yaquis. Returning to the river and headed south toward Onaves and then La Dura, the Rangers had encountered a battered, bloodied Mexican cavalry troop that had sustained severe losses from a recent fight with a Yaqui war party. Bloody and haggard, the Mexican officer warned them against continuing their journey south. Elliott thanked him, but insisted on the Rangers completing their mission. The tired Mexican officer only shook his head, saluted Elliott, and then took the troop north, leaving the four Rangers in the quiet, still afternoon alongside the *Rio Yaqui*.

The undulating countryside and accompanying vegetation obscured a clear view of the old Ranger but from time to time, Joaquin could see Elliott riding out ahead of them. Several coatimundi scurried away in front of him. Hickey and Shute rode behind with their .30-.40 Winchester rifles over the pommels of their saddles. They all knew vigilance was the key to their survival if they were to stay alive.

Viewing the fertile river valleys and meadows as he rode along, Joaquin now fully understood why the Mexican government wished to take it from the Yaqui Indians. They were natural farm lands and could easily sustain any crop desired. *Wheat would grow well here. I reckon life's hard sometimes and not always fair in this world we live in.*

He felt a hard tug on the lead rope from behind, the rope taut across this upper thigh. Over time the rope had formed a groove in his leather chaps. Agitated, he looked back over his shoulder at the contrary pack animals. "*Come on*, ya dang mules!" He spurred his paint horse into an easy trot; the two mules responded by trotting forward and not pulling back as before. Suddenly, the sound of rifle shots reverberated up the canyon from Elliott's point position. Then yelling, more shots in the distance.

Hickey shouted from behind, "What the hell?"

Joaquin reined his paint horse sharply around, spurring him into a hard run northward, back in the direction they had come.

"Dick ... Gene! This way!" he shouted over his shoulder as he headed for the thick grove of cottonwood trees they had ridden through moments before. All three rode hard, dismounting quickly as they reached the safety of the trees. Joaquin glanced quickly at Shute, and threw him the lead rope for the mules. "Secure the mules, Gene. We may need these supplies before this is over." Shute reached for the lead rope as the mules bucked and pitched.

Withdrawing his rifle from the saddle scabbard, Joaquin flipped the adjustable sights up on his .30-.40 1895 Winchester as he peered toward the open riparian area to the south. He could now see Elliott astride Viento, riding hard at a gallop toward the Rangers' new position. Then he saw the mounted Yaquis behind him—a dozen or more on either side. *They're trying to outflank him!* Joaquin heard more shots, yelling and screaming from the Yaqui warriors, who were closing on their prey.

The old Ranger leaned way forward in the saddle, his head close to Viento's neck as he gave the *grulla* plenty of slack in the reins. It appeared to Joaquin the two were gaining the lead on their pursuers, slowly but methodically increasing their ground. *Yeah! Out run 'em, Viento!* He felt his heartbeat quicken; he licked his dry lips, clutching the rifle tightly. *You can do it, boy!*

He yelled out to the other Rangers near him, "Use your adjustable sights, boys. Start shootin' when they get closer!" Kneeling down behind a large cottonwood tree, he under the quiet, panting gray bay. His paint horse, although ground-tied, shied back a ways from all the carnage. Solo Vino approached cautiously, and circled the dying horse; a low moan escaped from the dog's throat.

As Joaquin knelt beside the old horse, he heard Elliott say, "Ol' Viento ... why, I reckon he's plumb all in, *mijo.*" There was emptiness, hollowness in his voice. "He was the *best* pard a man could ever have."

Elliott removed the saddle with difficulty from the now still horse, then the bridle. Kneeling, the old Ranger looked across his faithful horse at Joaquin. The blue eyes were hard and sad. Releasing the air slowly from his lungs, he said, "Go an' ketch me one o' them Injun ponies, will ya, son?" He swallowed hard, bared his white head of hair as he removed his old gray Stetson. He leaned in close, peering into the horse's eyes as he stroked the bay's neck.

Nodding, Joaquin stood, a lump in his throat. As he walked toward one of the Indian ponies standing nearby, a loud report from Elliott's pistol made him jump. He sobbed quietly as he grasped the Indian pony's bridle tightly, attempting to hold on to the skittish horse.

Joaquin heard Elliott sigh deeply and say softly, a sad reverence in his deep voice, "Wel-l-l ... I reckon ... summer's over."

CHAPTER NINETEEN

Carmen awoke, feeling a cool breeze through the open window of her bedroom. The yellow sunlight filtered in slowly and began to illuminate the interior of the small room. She lay very still, her head nestled in the soft pillow, enjoying the early morning sounds. A mourning dove called out; several other doves cooed as they played amongst the thick foliage of the cottonwood trees lining the banks of Cienega Creek. A rooster crowed, a hungry dogie calf bawled out, then the silence returned.

She sighed, turning toward the small boy lying beside her. *Valgamé. Diós. My son has grown so big in just a year.* Lou looked a lot like his father. Dark brown hair, pretty brown eyes, and a ready smile for his mother. Carmen's eyes moistened as she thought of Joaquin. Where was he? Somewhere in Mexico—only God knew where. She had no way of knowing if he were alive, dead, or seriously injured. If something happened to him, would she ever know? *God! I hate him working with the Rangers!*

Carmen sat up in bed swinging her legs over the side of the bed. *I won't cry again. I won't!* As she stood, the long cotton night gown unfolded from her lap. She looked out the front window and seeing her father walking from the barn with a pail of milk, a smile came to her distraught face. Eagerly, she strode to the door, opened it and stepped out onto the porch of the old house.

"*Papa!*"

Domingo Ponce stopped and turned, a smile forming on his dark, weather beaten face. *"Bueños días, mi'ja."*

He walked to where she stood on the porch, set the heavy milk pail down, and climbed the two steps. His hair had turned completely white and his shoulders stooped where they once were squared. It had been several years since he narrowly escaped murder at the hands of Indio Chacon's rustlers. His employer Lou Campbell had not been so lucky.

"I'll feed the chickens, father," Carmen told him in Spanish. "It's something I can do while carrying Lou, and I want to help with the chores."

"As you wish." He held her close then released her, smiling again. *"Señora* Campbell asked that we eat breakfast with her at the ranch house this morning."

It was Carmen's turn to smile. "How nice of Marian! I'll get Lou and be right there."

She dressed and then straightened her hair in the small mirror in the bedroom. *Oh, my God. I look dreadful.* Her eyes were red and swollen from crying with dark circles underneath. Sighing, she quickly turned from the mirror, picked up her son, and headed out to the main ranch house a short distance away.

Cradling her son in her right arm, she lifted the metal latch on the old wooden door to the Campbell ranch house. The door creaked as it swung inward. The pleasant smell of bacon frying entered her nostrils. Her father sat at the table. An elderly woman turned from the wood cook stove and smiled broadly. Her white hair was tied up in a bun on her head, wisps of white dangled over her furrowed brow. The older woman's sun darkened face lit up at the sight of the younger woman.

"Mornin', Carmen. Come on over here and give this ol' lady a *big* hug."

They hugged, and Carmen said, "Thank you, Marian. For having us over for breakfast."

Marian Campbell gazed at her daughter-in-law for a moment and turned back toward the stove. She said, "You put lil' Lou down an' have a seat at the table. Breakfast is ready." The bacon in the skillet sizzled and spat grease as she turned it with a fork.

Carmen's son crawled a ways after being placed on the wood floor, then he stood and walked several tentative steps before falling. He looked back over his shoulder at his mother as if pleased with himself. Carmen smiled at him. "Wow, what a *big* boy!"

The adults sat quietly at the table, ate eggs, bacon, and tortillas and washed it all down with hot coffee. During her lifetime, Carmen had always noticed the conversation dwindle as folks ate a good meal. She reached down to her son and handed him a piece of tortilla. He grinned as he took the food and said clearly, "Ma ... ma."

"*Mi'jo,*" she replied affectionately.

Marian Campbell pushed her plate away and sipped from her coffee cup. "Carmen. I asked you here so's I could talk to ya an' your daddy at the same time."

Carmen pushed away her plate of partially eaten food. She looked quizzically at her mother-in-law. "Is there something wrong, Marian? Did I—?"

"No. Not that-away. What I mean is, well, I'm plumb worried 'bout you as of late."

"No cause to worry, Marian. I'm fit as a fiddle, as Elliott says." She laughed a short laugh then looked down at her unfinished breakfast.

Frowning, Marian leaned forward onto the kitchen table, her hazel eyes gazing directly at Carmen. Softly, she said, "No, I reckon not, honey. You've not been fit fer a spell, an' it ain't hard to see it."

"I *don't* want to talk about it." Carmen stood.

The soft voice of the elderly woman spoke again. "Please. Sit down."

Carmen closed her eyes, and sobbing, buried her face in her hands. Her mother-in-law stood and walked around the table to take the young woman into her arms. *Oh, Marian, I love you so.* The sobbing transitioned into crying out loud. Marian held her more closely, saying nothing. Domingo Ponce sat at the table; a painful expression appeared on his wrinkled face, but he said nothing.

Eventually, Carmen spoke between sobs. "I .. *hate*... him ... being gone all the time." She started to cry again then somehow stopped. "He's *never* here. And when he is ... all we ever do is fight!" Gulping for air, she continued, "We haven't slept together for months and we never talk anymore. I hate it all! Marian, I—" She released all the air from her lungs, sighed and closed her eyes again. Her face was numb.

"I know. I know, child. Sometimes, life jest don't seem fair."

"It's *not!*" Carmen cried out.

"There, there, child. Let's sit you down, an' I'll draw up a chair an' tell you a story."

"A ... a story?"

Marian helped Carmen sit in the wicker chair then selected another and sat next to her. She looked over at Domingo. He nodded solemnly. The elderly woman started to speak then hesitated before continuing, "It seems like many a year ago thet Elliott showed up here at the ranch— he jest showed up outta the blue—we hadn't heerd hide nor hair from 'im fer a long spell. It was 1898 as I recollect an' the Spanish American War had jest broke out." She rearranged the light wisps of white hair back from her forehead.

"He wanted *my* Lou to ... to go with him over to Cuba an' fight them Spaniards." Marian's tongue wet her

dry lips, first one side of her mouth then the other. "An'
Lou, he thinks fer a minute or two. Then he says, 'I reckon
so.'"

"He reckoned so!" she shouted. "What was he a
thinkin'? He had two kids an' a wife to care fer, a ranch thet
was barely making it with all of us a workin' hard to make
do."

Her hazel eyes blazing, Marian stood with her hands
on her hips. She looked down at Carmen and into her big,
brown eyes. Carmen brushed away residual tears. She said
between sobs, "What did you do?"

"I told Lou he was a *damn* fool, an' when he wouldn't
listen to me, I quit talkin' to him. Treated him like he wasn't
there." Carmen nodded her head. *Serves him right!*

"Then what happened?"

Marian looked into Carmen's eyes. "We quit talkin'
... an' bein' man an' wife. You know—sleepin' together.
He went off to war with it bein' like thet between us. You
know, without us makin' up atall." She sat down heavily in
the chair. "He wasn't gone all thet long, but long 'nough
fer me to realize thet if something had happened to 'im, I
could never forgive myself fer not makin' up afore he left."
She took Carmen's hands in her own. "Do you understand
what I'm sayin', child?"

"Yes. I think I do, Marian." Carmen bit at her lower
lip.

"Good fer you, Carmen."

"But Joaquin. If I never see him again. What if he
never returns?" Carmen's voice choked with emotion.

"He'll be back all right, honey. He's with Elliott."
Marian's eyes hardened then softened. "Thet damn gunman took my Lou from me an' over to Cuba, an' I *never*
forgave him fer thet. But he damn sure brought him back
after saving his life. Some men jest have a knack at bringin'

others back outta trouble."

"Oh, Marian. I *hope* so. I miss my Joaquin so." *He's got to come back to me.* Carmen wrung her hands. "But he won't *ever* leave the Rangers. He just won't quit!"

Carmen's mother-in-law sighed, looked out the window of the little ranch house. "I don't want to sound mean to you, Carmen, but if you two *always* fight, never talk, never be husband an' wife together, hate each other, why would he want to come home, to thet?"

"*Marian!*"

"You think 'bout it, honey. I know I did years ago with my Lou, Gawd rest his soul. You gotta decide what's best fer you an' your son. You jest remember Joaquin's providin' good money fer all of us from thet Ranger salary."

Carmen stood, looked at her father. He stood next to her then took her into his arms. "*Tiene razon, mi'ja.* She ees right."

She shrugged free from his embrace, picked up the baby, and made her way across the silent room outside to the porch. Tears streamed down her face; she dabbed at them with her free hand, not making much headway at drying her face. *God, help me do what's right. Please!*

Thunderclouds were building over the Whetstone Mountains; she could feel the change in humidity. Maybe they would get some much needed rain. Fall would be here soon. Lou struggled in her arms, wanting down. She set him down on the porch and watched the young boy finally stand on his own and walk several steps before toppling over. *Oh, Lou, I need your father as much as you do.* She sighed, straightening her shoulders. Her father and Marian needed help with the ranch work. There were chores to do; chickens to be fed.

CHAPTER TWENTY
Sonora, Mexico, September 1907

A s the Rangers rode out of La Dura, Joaquin dallied the lead rope for the pack mules around the saddle horn and touched his spurs lightly to the paint's flanks. He hastened to catch up with Elliott and the other two Rangers ahead of him. They had thoroughly searched La Dura and found that Gonzalez and Ascencion had left the small village just ahead of them, allegedly to work on a spur railroad track being built across a deserted stretch of Sonora.

Riding eastward, following the spur track after a hard day's ride, Joaquin could see the western approach of the Sierra Madre Mountains. He remembered his search several years earlier for the bandit Indio Chacon in those same steep, treacherous mountains but to the north of their present position. Chacon had murdered his father on their ranch, and with Elliott's help, the Rangers tracked him into Mexico and brought him back to be charged in the murder. It seemed so long ago. After a lengthy trial, the authorities found him guilty and hanged him. Chacon was one of the Arizona Territory's most nefarious outlaws. *Justice served! But killing the sumbitch never brought my Dad back to me.*

Joaquin rode his paint horse up to where Elliott, Hickey, and Shute sat on their horses under a large mesquite tree, the pack mules in tow acting relieved for a little rest. Elliott swung his right leg over the horn and pommel of his saddle, reached in his pocket for the can of Prince

Albert tobacco and papers.

"Take a looksee yonder, *mi'jo*, to the east. At the base o' thet *loma*."

Elliott quickly built his cigarette, licked the paper and placed it in the corner of his mouth. Striking a match with his thumb, he lit the cigarette, inhaling deeply. The Yaqui Indian pony he was riding stamped his foot impatiently. Elliott did not appear to notice.

Joaquin peered eastward toward a small hill bordering the majestic Sierra Madres on the west. A thin spiral of barely distinguishable smoke appeared on the horizon. He rubbed his jaw feeling the rough, week long stubble of beard on his face. The sunset had brightened the desert landscape behind them just moments before it had disappeared. Darkness would be upon them soon.

Elliott spoke. "I figger we'll camp here—no fires. Then we'll ease up on the camp after dark and ketch them *lowdown*, murderin' sumbitches." He grinned broadly at the three Rangers facing him. "What do you fellers think 'bout thet?"

"What if them killers make a fight of it? We still get the *re*ward?" asked Hickey.

"Dead or alive, I reckon," replied Elliott. "I figger on all o' us making it home safe. Them too, if they behave." He drew again on the cigarette, then tucked it in the corner of his mouth as he swung his leg back over the pommel and his foot into the stirrup on the right side. "If we take 'em alive, I want 'em searched *pronto*. Don't trust them no good sumbitches, ya hear?"

Only Joaquin responded, "Yes sir."

***

The small sliver of a moon provided barely enough light for Joaquin to discern the sleeping camp in front of him. He squatted behind a mesquite tree with Hickey beside him. The Rangers tied their horses and pack mules a ways back, then quietly approached the camp on foot— he and Hickey from the south and Elliott and Shute from the east. If shooting occurred, they would not be shooting across at each other. Elliott told Joaquin to get into position as close as possible without being detected. He felt Hickey stir next to him in the darkness as he drew his .45 Colt revolver, peering at the men sleeping near the smoldering campfire. A light breeze occasionally fanned the fire, briefly illuminating the blanketed sleeping forms on the ground. He would follow orders and wait for Elliott's signal.

Joaquin's eyes strained for movement from the sleeping men. His palms were sweating; he re-arranged his grip on the six-shooter. He counted eight men. *They must not be worried—no lookouts posted.* Would Gonzalez and Ascencion be among these railroad laborers? Elliott felt certain of it. One of the sleeping men stirred, turning over on his side. Several others snored loudly. A coyote howled mournfully in the clear night. None of its kind answered the call.

The quietness of the desert was suddenly shattered. "Git outta them blankets, you sumbitches! *Manos arriba!*" Elliott's voice thundered commands in English and Spanish. Befuddled men sat up abruptly to face Elliott and Shute with guns drawn just out of the light of the campfire. Joaquin and Hickey scrambled to their feet and stepped toward the fire, pointing their six-shooters at the disheveled men, some with hands in the air.

"*Damn you! Levántense—todos!*" The men stood as instructed, blankets falling to their feet. Reluctantly, the rest raised their hands. Elliott stepped closer. He pointed his revolver at a heavyset man who had a large ugly scar on the right side of his face. "*¿Comprende ingles, cabrón?*" asked

Elliott.

The powerful man shifted his thick-set arms. He grinned arrogantly at the old Ranger displaying a missing front tooth. *"No comprendo."*

Ranger Shute shouted, "He's a damn liar, Elliott. What's more, he's a dead ringer for Gonzalez, I tell ya."

"I kinda had the same idée," returned Elliott. "Holster thet pistol, step up and cuff 'im." He spoke to Joaquin and Hickey without turning, "Keep an eye peeled on them others. They move, shoot 'em."

Shute moved next to the big Mexican and placed heavy metal handcuffs on his wrists. He looked up into two dark, deep-set beady eyes. "You son-of-a-bitch. You'll pay for killing my kin."

The Mexican grinned, saying nothing.

Elliott said, "Shut up, Shute. You damn well know better'n cuffin' him in front. Chrissake! Search him! How many times I gotta tell ya?"

Shute began his search of the suspect, starting with his shirt pockets then his waist. Elliott turned to Joaquin, "Find out which of them others is Ascencion." He looked at a small man standing in the center of the others with their hands raised. "I'll wager he's our man." He turned back to Shute, who stood beside the powerful Mexican.

"You finished searching, Gene?"

"Yes sir. Look what I found in his belt in back." He held an old revolver in his hand.

"Good job. Now cuff 'im in back like you shoulda done in the first place."

Shute tossed the old revolver to the ground where Elliott was standing, then he used his key, unlocking one side of the cuffs. He said to the Mexican in Spanish, "Place your hands behind you, Gonzalez."

The Mexican hesitated, started to comply then

swiftly swung the arm with the heavy handcuffs, hitting Shute flush in the face. Blood flowed as Shute staggered backward. The powerful Mexican leapt behind the injured Ranger, placing him between Elliott and himself. He reached down with his right hand and pulled a concealed knife from inside his boot top. Grasping Shute around the neck, he drove the sharp blade hard into the Ranger's back between the ribs. He stabbed again and twisted the blade. Shute screamed.

Elliott moved quickly to the side, shooting at the part of the Mexican's head that was visible. The .45 revolver bucked in his hand. The big Mexican screamed, losing his grip on the young Ranger's neck, his left ear shot off.

"Damn your murderin' hide." Elliott shot him in the right eye, the back of his head exploding. Turning swiftly to the other prisoners, Elliott leveled his revolver at the smaller man he had indicated earlier. Breathing hard between clenched teeth, he said, "You Ascencion, uh?"

The small Mexican did not speak. Elliott's voice rasped with a metallic ring, "Don't reckon I'll be askin' agin." He cocked his six-shooter.

The man swallowed hard and shouted, "*Si, señor!* Plees don't shoot. I am Ascencion."

Joaquin stammered, "I'll check on Gene."

"I think it's too late fer 'im, *mi'jo*," returned Elliott, "but you go on an' help him if ya kin." He spoke sharply to Ranger Hickey, "Cuff this sumbitch *behind*. Then strip an' search 'im."

Hickey stood still, unable to move.

Breathing hard, sweating in the cool desert air, Elliott cleared his throat as he gazed at Hickey. "If I find anything on 'im, so much as one o' them Texas chiggers when you're done, I'll shoot *you!*"

Hickey moved hesitantly toward the small Mexican

man.

Joaquin knelt close to Gene Shute, who was struggling on the desert floor. Blood poured from his mouth. He choked then grimaced. "That ... dirty, murderin'—" He coughed, spewing blood on his shirt. Joaquin said nothing, holding Shute's bloodied hands.

Shute spoke again. "Joaquin ... you ... give ... my share of the *re*ward ... to my mama, you hear?" His body shaking uncontrollably, he whispered, "That dirty ... low-down—" The trembling ceased and Shute gave up his last gasp of breath.

Joaquin stood. His white face betrayed the shock of the previous violence. "Gene's gone." He looked over at the old Ranger. "The Mexican's dead, too."

"Just as well fer the *Mexicano*, I reckon. *Era un hombre muy malo.* He'd been trouble fer us all the way back home." Elliott kicked at the sandy soil with the toe of his boot. "I'm shore sorry 'bout Gene, son. Real sorry."

Elliott turned to the other frightened men in the railroad work crew and told them in Spanish, "We'll take Ascencion an' Gonzalez's body with us, but first we'll bury our dead Ranger friend." His voice rose, "Well, don't jest *stand* there lollygaggin', git shovels. You're helping dig!"

CHAPTER TWENTY-ONE

Carmen leaned against the corral poles, watching a dark young man wearing a large gray sombrero stalk the horses in the corral. He paused in his stride and swung the rope from his left hip, up and over his head; the soft hoolahand throw settled around a bay horse's head. The horse fought the rope momentarily then settled down for his handler as he was led from the corral. Carmen's father Domingo opened the gate for the young man as he led the horse out to the hitch rack. *"Que bien, Fernando."*

The young man smiled at his *jefe*, his face lighting up at the praise. Tall and slender for a *Mexicano*, he was dark complected with short coal black hair. He wore a rough cotton work shirt, pants, and worn riding boots. Strapped onto the boots were Mexican spurs with large rowels. The spurs jingled musically as he walked.

Carmen thought he was maybe twenty-five years old, if that. He had shown up one day at the ranch several months ago and asked for work for little pay. With Marian and Domingo overworked and unable to do the heavy ranch work, they both agreed to hire him at least until Joaquin could come home to assist. Fernando had been most appreciative of the opportunity and the meager wages. He worked hard, said very little even though Carmen had attempted to find out more about him.

He did tell her he was married, and his wife and daughter lived in the state of Sonora, Mexico. His dark eyes twinkled at the mention of family members. She knew nothing else of him as he kept mostly to himself at the barn where he slept.

Fernando placed a bridle with a curb bit on the bay, removed the lariat, and tied the horse securely to the hitch rack.

"Nan-do!" The young Mexican turned sharply toward the little boy standing in the shade of a large cottonwood tree. Nearly two years old, Lou walked fairly well on his own. Fernando smiled broadly at him as he watched the boy come to him, teetering on his small feet.

"*Lou, mi'jo! Venga aquí... a su amigo Nando, uh?*"

Carmen smiled as she watched her son hug the tall vaquero as he knelt to return the affection of the small boy. He spoke in Spanish, the small boy seemed to understand. "I have much work to do today, my little friend." Patting Lou on his small shoulders, he stood, looking down at him. "How are you this fine morning?"

The boy smiled. "*Mooy bíen, Nan-do.*"

"Veery goot," replied the vaquero. Then he laughed out loud.

"Lou, come here please." Carmen walked toward her son, smiling. "Let Nando get back to work, *mi'jo.*" Lou turned to his mother, toddling toward her. "O-kay, Mommy."

Fernando looked at Carmen. She wore a plain blue cotton blouse and skirt. Her black, glossy hair was braided into two braids, hanging down her back. She smiled at him, her pretty, brown face with those sad, brown eyes. He stared momentarily at her; his face flushed, and he averted his eyes, looking at the ground. He spoke again in Spanish, "And how are you, Carmen?"

"I'm fine, Fernando. Thank you for spending time with my son. He needs a man's attention."

Fernando did not look up. "He is a good boy. His

father will be home soon."

Carmen's face flushed, and she averted her eyes. "Yes. God willing. Joaquin will return to us."

"Hasta luego, señora."

Holding Lou's little hand, Carmen watched Fernando walk quickly to the corral where her father stood waiting. *There's a good man who loves his family. Just like me, he's lonely.* She reached down and lifted Lou into her arms. Her emotions got the better of her as she turned toward the ranch house. *God, please, please bring my Joaquin home safely to me. I love him. And don't let me be so hateful to him when he comes.*

The day passed uneventfully for Carmen. As evening approached, she prepared supper for her father and Lou. Her son was tired, nearly falling asleep before he finished eating. She tucked him into bed and gave him a kiss on the forehead. His little eyes fluttered then closed as he gave way to much needed sleep.

Carmen returned to the kitchen, finished washing and drying the dishes. She turned, carrying the dish pan full of water and walked outside to edge of the porch. Carefully, she flung the dishwater out onto the dry desert floor; the moisture instantly disappeared from the surface. Holding the empty dishpan, she stood for a moment peering out into the darkness. *What is it?* She sensed something in the night but saw nothing. Finally, she shrugged, turned and re-entered the ranch house.

***

Across the creek adjacent to a large cottonwood tree, a pair of sad dark brown eyes watched as Carmen stood quietly on the porch. The eyes softened as they carefully observed the young woman. The young man's face was filthy; a week's growth of dark beard covered his deeply tanned face. Thick dust clung to his range clothes, leather chaps and boots. His jaw was set hard, clenching his teeth as he stared at the woman, breathing hard; he reached up and pulled the sweat-stained, brown Stetson further down onto his head.

He saw the woman turn to go back inside. *No! Don't go. Not just yet, Carmie.* The door to the ranch house opened, emitting light from within, then closed returning the porch to inky darkness.

Joaquin sobbed silently in the darkness, his eyes tightly closed. He took a deep breath of the cool night air, squared his shoulders, turned, and walked back to his paint horse some quarter of a mile distant. He mounted quickly, called softly into the night, "Sol. Boy?" The old black and white dog appeared from nowhere. Joaquin's voice was full of sadness. "Nothing here for me anymore, boy." He reined the horse east toward Bisbee. "Nothing but fighting, and I reckon I can do without that." He touched his spurs lightly to the paint's flanks.

CHAPTER TWENTY-TWO
Benson, Arizona Territory
February, 1908

Joaquin Campbell took another sip of coffee then scooted his wooden chair back from the restaurant table to be more comfortable. He had met Wheeler at the Virginia Hotel to discuss potential leads on the Calhoun and Mexican prostitute's deaths in Naco and to obtain further orders. However, his boss was complaining about territory politics.

"Damned politicians!" Wheeler spewed across the table as he reached for his coffee cup. He took a big gulp of hot coffee, set the cup down. "They're bound and determined to undo all the good work we've done for the past seven years."

Joaquin shifted forward with his elbows on the table. "Who is, Cap'n?"

"The Democrats have been taking control of the two-house legislature, son. They already outnumber the Republicans in the Council ten to two, and they're working hard on increasing their numbers in the House of Representatives."

Joaquin frowned. "What does that have to do with us?"

"The Democrats, especially O'Neill and Weedin, have been pushing for several years to repeal the Ranger Act and abolish the Arizona Rangers," said Wheeler heavily.

"Why ... for God's sake? Aren't we doing what the territory wants done?" countered Joaquin.

Wheeler sighed. "We were created by a Republican Governor and the Ranger Act was passed by a Republican legislature. The Democrats will never forgive that, son."

"I just don't understand it atall," returned Joaquin.

"Well, it's for me to deal with, I reckon. Governor Kibbey says he doesn't think they'll be able to override his veto even if a bill does pass to abolish us." Licking his lower lip, he said, "But enough of dirty politics—what about the Calhoun case? Any new leads?"

"No sir. I still haven't figured out what Bill was trying to tell us when he scrawled whatever he scrawled in blood on the floor."

"Did Elliott talk to you about his theory of Bill using one finger at a time or three together to write that message in blood?" asked Wheeler.

Joaquin repositioned himself in his chair. "Yessir. And I agree with him. It's just hard to figger if the letters were all the same—you know, made with three fingers together. I talked with the coroner, and he said both of Bill's hands were pretty much covered in blood when he examined him."

Wheeler nodded while frowning. "That's too bad."

Pursing his lips, Joaquin eagerly said, "If I could only find the man with the right foot boot that's built up on the outside of the heel."

Wheeler smiled. "Well, you keep looking, son. We'll find him. You just remember perseverance and patience is needed for good detective work, uh?"

Their conversation was interrupted by the owner of the hotel as he approached their table. "Harry," the man began.

"What is it Eduardo?"

Eduardo Castañeda placed his thumbs in his vest pockets before he spoke with a frown. "There may be trouble at the train depot."

Wheeler stood, reaching for his hat. "What kind of trouble?" He placed his flat-brimmed hat squarely on his head. Joaquin pushed back his chair and stood next to Castañeda.

Castañeda leaned in close to both Rangers. "A couple—man and woman—stayed at the hotel last night." He peered at Wheeler. "Anyhow, the man just asked me for a gun. Said a man named Tracy was outside and intending to kill him and the woman."

"You believe him?"

"There's a man seated on the steps at the east side of the train depot."

"You see a gun?" asked Wheeler.

"Nope. But he's wearing a coat. Could have several."

"Okay Eduardo. I'll check it out. The couple still in their room?"

"I think so."

"*Bueno.*" You keep 'em there. I'll check out the man at the depot."

Castañeda hurried up the stairs to find the couple. Wheeler turned to Joaquin. "Your horse tied up outside?"

"Yessir."

"You'd best head out, son; get on down to Naco and work the border with Sergeant Kidder. I want those gun-runners caught and the sooner the better."

Joaquin hesitated. "You want me to help check out the feller across the street before I ride?"

"Naw. You get started; it'll be a long ride for you. This is most likely a lover's spat. I can handle it."

"Okay, Harry. I'll be on my way then." Joaquin paid

for his meal and walked outside to the paint horse tied to the hitch rack. Mounted, he reined the horse south onto San Pedro Street, glancing at a hatless man with his head down, slumped on the steps adjacent to the east side of the railway depot.

***

Captain Harry Wheeler stepped onto the board sidewalk in front of the Virginia Hotel. It was a bright, sunny winter day with a slight breeze. He peered across dusty Fourth Street at a man sitting near the east side the Southern Pacific Railroad train depot. He thought it strange the man was wearing a coat but no hat. Wheeler stepped down into the street, crossed it, and approached the solitary man. *Must be Tracey?* The man seemed oblivious to the lawman and was looking beyond him, toward the hotel.

Suddenly, the hatless man jumped up and began cursing loudly. Wheeler hesitated, turning toward the hotel. He saw another man with a woman standing on the sidewalk in front of the hotel. *Dammit! I told Eduardo to keep 'em in their room.* Turning back toward the hatless man, Wheeler saw in horror the man had drawn a revolver from his pocket. He swiftly drew his own .45 revolver, pointed it at the armed man.

"Hold it!" shouted Wheeler. "You're under arrest. Give me your gun!"

The man began firing his revolver wildly. Wheeler advanced, firing at his adversary, again ordering him to drop the gun. The Ranger Captain felt a hot searing pain in his upper thigh near his groin. He stumbled, then fired four rounds at the hatless man, striking him under the heart, neck, and thigh; knocking the man onto his back.

The man known as Tracey gasped, "My gun's empty."

Having fired all five shots, Wheeler dropped his revolver and limped forward to take custody of his prisoner.

Then he saw the man reloading his revolver with an extra two rounds from his pocket. Nothing else to do, Wheeler bent down and picked up a rock to throw at his treacherous adversary. As the man pointed his revolver at the Ranger Captain, two shots rang out almost instantaneously, and the hatless man was flung on his back. He did not move again.

Wincing with pain, Wheeler turned to see Ranger Joaquin Campbell lithely swing his right leg over the horn of his saddle and slide down to the dusty street with his .45 Colt revolver still smoking.

"You okay, Cap'n? I heard shots and came running."

"Thanks. Help me over to the hotel so I can take my breeches off and check this wound in my upper thigh, son." Frowning, he peered down at his blood-soaked pants near his groin, feeling blood run freely down the inside of his pants and into his boot top.

Grimacing, he swallowed hard, whistled low then said softly, "Another inch or two ... *valgamé*. I'd be talking with a helluva high-pitched voice."

CHAPTER TWENTY-THREE
Bisbee, Arizona Territory
Spring, 1908

The moonless night had settled. Elliott walked along the board sidewalk down Bisbee's main street, relying on infrequent street lights and his knowledge of the area from years past, his spurs clinking as he sauntered along.

He passed the Bank of Bisbee, and continued along the canyon and Main Street, stopping at the Orpheum Theatre. Elliott built a cigarette taking his time, lit it, and smoked quietly reminiscing events and old haunts of a past long ago.

Copper had been found in Mule Pass Gulch in 1875 and the Copper Queen Consolidated Mining Company had made a fortune from the ore deposits. Victorian residences were erected in the six-mile long canyon in 1901 and brick buildings lined Main Street with shoddy, framed shacks now precariously perched along the rocky canyon walls above. The pungent smell of wood smoke filled the air.

He tucked the cigarette in the corner of his mouth and turned left down mile-long Brewery Gulch. It was not the rough place it had been in its heyday, but it was still dangerous with its saloons, dance halls, brothels, gambling halls and all the folks that worked and frequented such raucous places. Elliott snorted. *No damned street in the territory could boast more sin than Brewery Gulch.*

It seemed an entire life time ago when his friend Hao Li had found him here in Bisbee—outside the Orient Saloon, drunk on rot-gut whiskey and doped up from smoking opium. He was barely alive and in the throes of hell and death warmed over after losing his first wife and son to the Apache several years before. The Chinaman had taken him in and nursed him back to health, showing him there was a lot more to life than hatred, killing, and feeling sorry for himself. *Godalmighty! How many years has it been now?*

Elliott wore his gray Stetson hat, range clothes, and an unbuttoned wool jacket. Beneath the jacket on the left side was a secured shoulder holster containing a .45 Colt revolver. He had chosen not to wear his gun belt, but he never went anywhere unarmed these days.

He walked on down the street, finally stopping in front of the Orient Saloon. Taking his time, he finished his smoke, dropped the butt to the sidewalk, and ground it out with his dusty boot. He stepped through the batwing doors, adjusting his eyes to the dimly lit interior of the smoke-filled saloon. Men were drinking at the bar; all the tables were full of men intent at playing cards, and standing room only was the order of the day. He shouldered his way through the crowd into the middle of the room, his eyes searching.

"Howdy, cowboy! Buy me a drink?"

The voice was close to him. He swung his gaze toward the female voice; the smell of cheap perfume filled his nostrils. His gaze settled on a saloon girl standing next to him wearing a gaudy, skimpy black dress. She smiled broadly showing large, white teeth. Her lips were painted red, and the make-up on her face had begun to run.

"Howdy yourself," Elliott said.

The woman pressed herself against him, displaying a large bosom, which was barely concealed in the tight dress. "You, uh, looking for some fun?" She had a deep throaty laugh. "Debra's my name, honey."

He moved a step backward, looking her over. "No, I reckon not. But I'll do better'n thet drink if you can tell me where a friend of mine is."

The woman pouted. "I might know of your friend's whereabouts."

"I figgered as much. He's a young feller, good lookin' boy, brown hair, 'bout six feet tall an' wears a brown Stetson." Elliott's blue eyes bored into the woman's eyes.

Her eyes wavered, looked down at the floor. "You're a mean, hard man ain't ya, mister?"

Elliott said nothing.

She cleared her throat. "I know where he is. He's been comin' here regular like lately."

Elliott reached in his pants pocket and handed her a five dollar bill. "Show me!"

Shouldering past the crowded patrons, she led the way up the stairs in the back of the saloon to one of the rooms. Smiling, she held the bill up to the light. "Hell, mister you wouldn't pay this much for *me*." She headed back down the stairs, stopped and turned. "You, uh, change your mind later?"

"I reckon not." Elliott opened the door without knocking.

The small dimly lit room barely had space for a cot and table; Joaquin Campbell lay passed out on top of the cot. Elliott stepped over to the wash basin sitting on a small table next to the bed. He picked up the water pitcher and tossed all its contents out onto the sleeping young Ranger.

Joaquin sprang up to sitting position. "What the ... *hell!*"

"Time to go home, *mi'jo*."

"Elliott?" Joaquin brusquely shook the cold water

from his face and hair, peering at the tall, white-haired man standing over him. "That you?"

"Yessir, I reckon so," the old Ranger drawled.

Standing up from the bed, Joaquin wavered. He sat back down suddenly. Leaning over, he placed his head between his knees while resting on his elbows. Elliott waited. Suddenly, Joaquin groaned and burped loudly. Moments passed.

Joaquin took a deep breath. "I ... can't ... *go* back home."

"Why the hell not?"

"I just *can't,* dammit," shouted Joaquin.

Elliott sat down heavily on the bed next to the young Ranger. "Let's you an' me take a looksee at this here sitiation." He frowned, his brow furrowing. "*You,*" Elliott said sharply as he jabbed Joaquin hard in the chest, "have a home, a family—a real purty wife and a son who, as I recall, loves you very much."

"No, not anymore. I—" Joaquin dropped his head again, closing his eyes.

Elliott's voice had a metallic ring in it. "You shut *the hell* up. I ain't finished talkin' here." He stood and jerked Joaquin's thick head of hair back upright. Holding it taut, he continued, "I'm *ashamed* of ya. Here in this ... this *goddamned* place! Where's your pride, boy? What the hell's the matter with you anyhow—feeling sorry fer yourself, uh?"

"Look, Elliott. I can explain—"

"I said, shut up!" The old Ranger let go of Joaquin's hair and turned away with his head down. He was quiet for several minutes. "Don't think I don't know this hyar place. I been here shore 'nough. Years ago. And it's as damned worthless and wicked now as it was back in them days."

He turned back, kneeling in front of Joaquin. He said softly, "Don't ya *see,* boy? This is no life fer you—fer

Lou Campbell's son. Christsake! Cain't ya *see* it? You have folks dependin' on you at home."

"I'm sick to death of fighting with Carmen. Every *single* day! She won't listen, just blows up."

"And lil' Lou? What o' him, uh?"

The icy words cut into Joaquin. "What can I do, Elliott? *What?*"

Elliott took a deep breath, released all the air from his lungs, and stood. "You kin be a man, *mi'jo*. Own up to your family *res*ponsibilities. Set down with Carmen—talk things out. Give her and the boy a hug or two."

"I'm not sure I can do that."

"Shore ya kin, boy," returned Elliott. He slapped Joaquin on the shoulder. "Come on, stand up. We're gittin' the hell outta here." He reached over to the bedside table for Joaquin's hat, jammed it down on his head then assisted him toward the door of the room. The old Ranger opened the door and faced Joaquin. The metallic ring was back in his voice. "You *ever* leave your family agin, an' come here, I'll tan your hide. *¿Comprende?*"

The younger man swallowed hard. "Yessir. I under-stand."

A smile worked at the corner of Elliott's mouth then disappeared. "Good boy. Thet's the Joaquin I remember! Let's go on home, *mi'jo*, uh?"

CHAPTER TWENTY-FOUR

It had been a long day. Carmen wearily brushed her dark hair back from her forehead and leaned down to tuck her son into his bed. Smiling, she watched his young face quietly burrow into the soft pillow. His little brown eye lids fluttered, then closed. *Que bonito, mi'jo. Te amo,* she thought as she blew out the kerosene lamp and softly pulled the bedroom door shut behind her.

She heated water on the wood cook stove and washed the supper dishes she and her father had used. Exhausted, she stepped out onto the porch of the small ranch house with her arms folded and took a deep breath, then released it slowly. The night air smelled fresh and clean, a small breeze rustled the hair near her forehead and pleasantly cooled her face. *What a beautiful evening!* They'd received spring showers two days previously, and the skies were cloudy for several days. Tonight the night sky was clear with no clouds in sight, the numerous stars twinkled down at her and the leaves of the cottonwood trees along the banks of Cienega Creek rustled in the wind. The smell of desert creosote accentuated the night air.

Suddenly, she realized she was not alone. She turned sharply to her left and seeing nothing, frowned, listening intently. *Yes! I hear it now. But what?* Spurs jingled in the night air. Startled, she turned abruptly to her right and saw two men approaching the ranch house, leading their horses. Her heart pounded as she peered more closely into the dark night. Then she recognized Joaquin's paint horse, the other as the Yaqui Indian pony Elliott had taken to riding lately. She swallowed hard then bit her lower lip. "Joaquin? Elliott? Is that you?"

A deep voice drawled out to her, "It shore is, Carmen. It's me an' Joaquin come home."

"*Valgamé!*" She clutched her throat, unable to move as the two men approached. Leaving their horses ground-tied, they stepped up on the porch close to her, their spurs clinking on the wooden steps. They both removed their hats and smiled at her. Joaquin appeared nervous; his smile disappeared as he glanced at her, then looked down at the ground.

"Well, don't jest stand there gawkin', Carmen. Give ol' Elliott a hug, doggone it."

Carmen hugged the old Ranger with all her might and began crying. He patted her softly, "Now, now. Everything's gonna be all right 'lil one," Elliott soothed. He grasped her gently by the shoulders and turned her toward Joaquin.

Joaquin swallowed hard, started to speak, stopped. He cleared his voice, "Carmie ... I ... uh ..."

Elliott interjected, "I reckon I'll leave you youngins alone." Descending the porch, he reached down and took the reins for both horses. Without turning, he said over his shoulder as he headed for the barn, "You jest be yourself, son, an' it'll be all right."

Joaquin fumbled with his hat; Elliott's spurs clinked loudly then the night became quiet. He dared to look at Carmen. She stood quietly on the porch with her arms near her sides. Her large brown eyes looked directly into his sad eyes. The evening breeze toyed with a wisp of hair near her forehead. She was dressed in a simple blue cotton dress that accentuated her slender feminine figure. Still she said nothing, only peered into his eyes then took all of him into her gaze, noting his clean-shaven appearance. Joaquin placed his injured left hand into his back pocket.

She smiled. "I'm glad you're home, Joaquin."

He dropped his hat as she opened her arms, and then he hugged and kissed her. He held her at arms length, sobbing. He embraced her again, tightly.

"Carmen. I love you so!"

Laughing, she struggled free from his tight grasp. "And I love you, my husband."

Joaquin swallowed hard, frowning. "The Rangers ... I —"

She stopped him with a finger on his lips. "You do what *you* feel is necessary for this family, Joaquin. If it's rangering, well, then I'll be here waiting for you when you come home."

"But I thought—"

Carmen placed her whole hand over his mouth. "Oh, don't misunderstand me, *mi querido*. I don't like the dangerous work you do. Just the thought of you dealing with those bad men scares me nearly to death, but it has to be *your* decision in the end—not mine."

He held her tightly in his arms again. "Thank you."

She continued, "I'll *never* stop worrying that you're hurt or ... dead out there in the middle of nowhere, and I'll never see you again." Sobbing, she placed her head against his chest. As they held each other neither of them spoke then she stammered, "And I don't intend to bring this subject up—ever again!"

"And little Lou, Carmen?"

Smiling again, she said, "He's well, and getting so *big*, Joaquin. He misses his father, too."

Joaquin's voice quavered. "I *love* you!"

She placed her arms around his neck, pulling him to her, and kissed him. Her lips parted slightly as she kissed him more passionately. Joaquin returned the kiss, then he kissed her hair, her neck, and pulled her tightly against him. They stumbled back on the porch, both of them laughing. It was like old times, and they were in love again for the first time in their lives.

Carmen reached down and took his left hand with the two missing fingers within hers. She kissed the hand as she gazed again into his eyes. "Come with me, my husband. We've a lot of catching up to do."

Holding hands, the young couple entered the old ranch house together; the rough wooden door creaked closed behind them. A quiet settled again over the desert landscape; an owl hooted in the distance as the clink of spurs disturbed the stillness of the night.

Elliott chuckled, "Wel-l-l ... doggoned if she didn't get the last word in on ya, *mijo*. Them women is like thet, I reckon."

CHAPTER TWENTY-FIVE

Deep rolling thunder roared in the dark night, followed by a brilliant flash of lightning illuminating the desert terrain dotted with tall saguaro cactus and billowing ocotillos; the wind began to increase in velocity out of the northwest. Joaquin Campbell pulled his Stetson down on his head and reached for the slicker tied to his saddle. Donning the slicker, he left it unbuttoned with easy access to his gun belt. His paint horse nickered, stamped his foot nervously and turned his rear toward the oncoming storm. In the distance, another horse nickered back at him. *Jeff Kidder's sorrel gelding having a say in things.*

Darkness again. A slow, steady rain fell not too hard at first, followed by a driving downpour that drenched the men and their horses waiting impatiently in the darkness. More thunder, closer this time—a loud *crack!* The lightning split the sky virtually in half. And more rain, incessant rain, flooded the arroyos, dampened the parched soil replenishing the water reserves for the drought resistant desert plants.

Joaquin missed Solo Vino. *Wish you were here, boy.* The dog was almost always at his side. He and Kidder had left both their dogs at the Ranger Station in Naco. Kidder's little dog Jip seemed to enjoy the older dog's company.

Joaquin hunkered down beneath a palo verde tree that allowed him some respite from the inclement weather. It rained hard continuously for about an hour, then stopped almost as suddenly as it began. He shivered under the rain slicker as a cool breeze passed, heading southeast, behind the main front of the storm. Standing under the tree, he stamped his cold feet and left the paint horse, proceeding a hundred yards to the mesquite tree he had previously determined to be a good location to wait for the outlaws. He knelt down, peering at the ground in front of him. Even with the recent heavy rainfall, he could easily discern the wagon wheel tracks in the soil. *Gun runners!*

The previous day, he and Sergeant Jeff Kidder of the Arizona Rangers had completed a reconnaissance of the border area east of Naco. It had been an easy task for them to find abundant evidence of someone using a heavily-loaded wagon while traveling back and forth from Mexico. Sergeant Kidder decided they would stake out the tracks and hopefully catch the perpetrators. Joaquin knew Kidder to be under a similar tree farther south of his location, within yards of the U.S.-Mexico border.

As Kidder felt a scout would be used in advance of the wagon, he advised Joaquin to let the scout on horseback pass through, allowing the wagon load of contraband to be positioned between the two Rangers. Joaquin was to confront the wagon. If the driver forced the team toward the border, Kidder would be waiting. It was a good plan, Joaquin thought, except they needed more Rangers. If the wagon was heavily guarded, two might not be enough.

However, there were only twenty-six Rangers, including officers, and all of them were spread thin throughout the territory. And there were no guarantees they would ever catch these gun runners. Joaquin had a good feeling in his belly about this particular stakeout.

He and Jeff Kidder had practiced shooting the day before, and he was proud of his accuracy and swiftness with his .45 Colt revolver. Not that he was close to Kidder in his shooting abilities. With Elliott gone from the Ranger ranks, Jeff Kidder was unequaled in his prowess with a handgun. He was the quickest draw and the best shot, bar none, and he could shoot equally well with either hand. They had tacked playing cards up on a mesquite tree and took turns drawing and shooting at each card. Kidder hit the card dead center three out of six times from thirty feet away and did so with either hand. Joaquin's draw was not as fast, and he didn't have the pin-point accuracy of his sergeant, but Kidder was impressed at how well the younger Ranger shot, and said as much.

What was that? Joaquin's breath quickened. He listened intently, straining to hear the slightest sound. Nothing. Then, the sound again? The small, subtle sound of ... then he recognized it. A horse tossing the bit in his mouth. The horse snorted. *They're coming!* Oh, how he wished he could let Kidder know. His heart racing, Joaquin took three breaths, holding each one momentarily then expelling the air. It helped to calm him down. *Thanks for the tip, Elliott.* He drew his six-shooter, stood behind the tree in the darkness and waited.

He saw the horse and rider first then he heard the heavily laden wagon lumbering behind. The rider was armed with a rifle, the butt resting against his thigh. He was vigilant, peering from side to side and stopping frequently to listen before advancing toward the border. Joaquin let him pass; feeling fortunate the man's horse was not alerted to his presence.

The young Ranger waited, clutching his revolver tightly. His heart pounded in his chest, his mouth was dry. The team of horses and wagon appeared suddenly out of the mist just as the scout had done. There were two men sitting in the buckboard wagon seat—one armed with a shotgun, the driver holding the reins with both hands. The wagon lumbered forward slowly, lurching from side to side on the rough, uneven ground.

Joaquin cocked his single-action Colt revolver, stepped out in front of the on-coming wagon, pointing the weapon at the man with the shotgun. "Arizona Rangers, hold it right there!" he barked.

The outlaw with the shotgun brought the weapon up to his shoulder; Joaquin fired twice. The man fell backward over the seat as he swung his handgun toward the driver. He heard shots fired near the border where Kidder had positioned himself. First a rifle. One shot. Then Kidder's .45 Colt, three shots. The driver leaned low in his seat, slapped the reins hard, yelling at the horses, urging them to run. Right at Joaquin! He snapped two quick shots at the driver and dove to his right as the team and wagon swept past, narrowly missing him, gathering speed, running for the border.

Joaquin hit the ground and rolled on his shoulder, then quickly leapt up from the ground. He ran hard and dove headlong at the wagon, barely able to grasp the back end of the heavy buckboard. Dragged behind the wagon, he began losing his grip. Summoning all his strength, he slowly pulled himself up toward the wagon, straining all the muscle and sinew in his upper body. Joaquin almost made it up to the back of the wagon. The wagon bounced hard, he slipped and fell back to merely hanging on and was again dragged through the desert.

The muscles in his arms strained, ached and burned to the breaking point. He almost released his tight grasp on the back of the wagon. Methodically and with great difficulty, he finally pulled his body up and onto the back of the bouncing wagon. The wagon was fully loaded with a tarp covering the contents. The driver was yelling in Spanish at the team of horses, urging them on, faster south toward the Mexican border. The wagon suddenly hit a rock, bounced again. Joaquin almost lost his hard-earned seat atop the wagon load.

Carefully and slowly, he crawled toward the driver. Hatless, he sweated profusely under his ripped rain slicker. Nearing the driver, he drew his additional .45 Colt revolver from a shoulder holster beneath his left armpit. He brought the barrel down hard along the man's skull. The driver slumped forward, and Joaquin guided him down into the buckboard seat, after re-holstering his six-shooter. A chilly wind whipped at his exposed face as the team charged ahead into the cold, wet darkness. Joaquin slid into the driver's seat, and after some searching, found the reins for the team of horses.

"Whoa! Whoa now!" he screamed at the top of his lungs as he pulled back hard on the reins.

The team began to slow their speed then stopped, heaving and snorting in the still desert night. Spooked, they began moving again with Joaquin bringing them back into compliance with the tension on the reins. "Stop, dammit! *Stop!*" he gasped. His chest heaved, burned; he found it difficult to breathe as he sat on the driver's seat of the buckboard. His adrenaline-laden body shook uncontrollably.

Sergeant Kidder's voice echoed out into the night, "You all right?"

Joaquin stammered, "Yeah ... I ... reckon."

Kidder appeared near the wagon leading a horse with a bloody saddle. "Good work, kid."

"Where are we, Jeff?"

Laughing, Kidder returned, "Some damn place east of Naco and a ways down into *Mexico*, I reckon." He looked around in the darkness. "Don't rightly know for sure, Joaquin."

"The scout?"

"Deader'n a doornail, I'd say," quipped Kidder.

"I fired at the shotgunner twice," said Joaquin, looking over at the prostrate man and pointing to him lying in the buckboard. "This one here, I clubbed on the head. Don't know if he's alive or not."

Kidder tied the horse to a nearby palo verde tree. "Well, set the brake and tie the reins up so we can see what's in the wagon."

Joaquin did as he was instructed by the senior officer. Carefully, he searched the man lying across the wagon seat. After finding a six-shooter and a knife, he tossed them as far as he could out into the desert. Then he assisted Kidder in peeling back the heavy tarp on top of the wagon load.

Kidder whistled shrilly. The spooked horses moved suddenly, the wagon lurched forward for several feet, almost knocking Joaquin off to the ground. "*Hoo wee*. Land-sake! Lookee here, kid!"

The heavy wagon was fully loaded with wooden boxes of what appeared to be thousands of rounds of ammunition. Other boxes were marked as containing rifles and handguns.

"We done hit pay dirt, Joaquin." Grinning, Kidder looked up at the young Ranger. "We best get the wagon and this confiscated load outta *Mexico* into the good ol' USA and on to the Ranger Station in Naco."

"You reckon the smugglers will send someone to check on this load not getting through?" Joaquin asked.

"Yep, but we'll be long gone, *amigo*."

The Rangers loaded the bodies of the shotgunner and scout onto the wagon and revived the driver who turned out not to be dead as early morning light penetrated the dark, cloudy southwestern sky. Joaquin cuffed the bandit driver behind his back and left him on the buckboard seat. He found his own paint horse and tied him to the back of the wagon as Kidder did the same with the scout's horse.

Kidder offered him a drink from his canteen. Joaquin's mouth had been dry for way too long. He drank heartily, water running down his chin and neck.

"Hey, don't drink it all!" Kidder laughed as he jerked the canteen away from Joaquin.

"Sorry." Joaquin wiped his chin with the back of his hand.

"No need to be." Kidder looked at the younger Ranger approvingly. "You did well tonight, Joaquin. You've developed into one helluva peace officer."

The famous Ranger didn't refer to him as a kid. His face flushed with pride.

Kidder drained the canteen and replaced the lid. "Say, did I tell you I've got a lead on Billy Calhoun's murder?"

"Nah. What happened?"

"I'm gonna meet a contact tomorrow—at a *cantina* just across the border in Naco, *Mexico*."

"Who is it?" asked Joaquin eagerly.

"Reckon I'll find out *mañana*." Kidder slipped his canteen strap over the saddle horn.

"But Cap'n Wheeler told us not to go across the border into Naco after that American was killed there two weeks ago," declared Joaquin.

"Yeah. Well, I'll slip over and back before the Cap'n figgers it out." He laughed. "You want to catch the bastard who killed Billy, don't ya?"

"More'n anything, Jeff."

"Well then, I'll find out who killed him. And then you and me, we'll go arrest the son-of-a-bitch." He smiled and slapped Joaquin on the back. "What ya say to that, uh?"

Joaquin's worried look was replaced with a broad smile. "I'd like that, Jeff. I'd like that a lot."

CHAPTER TWENTY-SIX
Fall, 1908

It was a bright, sunny afternoon with no clouds in the blue Arizona sky. Joaquin pulled his Stetson down low over his eyes as a light spring breeze rustled the dark green leaves of a Chinese elm tree along Sixth Street in Douglas, Arizona Territory. He felt good about life again. He and Carmen had mended their sour relationship, and he was elated in his love for her and his son Lou. His spurs clinked in unison with his partner's as they strode side by side down the board sidewalk near the Mexican border.

Ranger Frank Shaw was a tall, lean young man who hailed from Kansas. His brown Stetson covered a head of dark wavy hair. Today his hazel eyes looked worried to Joaquin. He stopped, looking directly at Joaquin. "Jeff Kidder is dead. He was shot to death down in Naco three days ago."

"*What?*" Joaquin stammered.

"It's true. Cap'n Wheeler is trying to get his body from the Mexicans."

"What ... happened?" Joaquin's voice sounded hollow.

Shaw frowned. "Best I can tell, Jeff was interviewing a Mexican gal in a *cantina* in Naco, Mexico. Two Mexican policemen kicked the door open and busted in; one of 'em shot Jeff in the belly. Jeff drew his .45 and killed 'em both, made a run for the border on foot with his little dog Jip."

Joaquin's mouth fell open. "*No.*"

Shaw looked steadily at his friend and fellow Ranger. "I'm afraid it's so, Joaquin. He made it as far as the border fence, but didn't have the strength to get through it. Mexican line riders came at him. He shot one outta the saddle, winged a couple others, but ran out of ammunition."

"My God. Poor Jeff." Joaquin swallowed hard and took a deep breath, releasing it slowly.

"They pinned a sign on him." Shaw grimaced. "Something about this is what happens to lawmen who interfere with border business."

"They did that? Put a *damn sign* on him like ... some *damn* criminal?"

"I reckon they did, Joaquin." Shaw looked away from his friend's blazing brown eyes. "Cap'n says he figgers the warning was for all of us, but you in particular." He shuffled his boots on the board sidewalk. "You know. Since you and Jeff confiscated that wagon load of weapons and 10,000 rounds of ammunition down near Naco."

Joaquin whistled low. "You reckon the gun runners are tied in with the Mexican police and line riders?"

"Cap'n thinks so. Money buys a lot in this ol' world, I'd say," replied Shaw.

Joaquin felt sick to his stomach. He sighed, closing his eyes. *Those dirty murdering sons-a-bitches.* A thought struck him. He turned suddenly toward Shaw. "What happened to his dog—to Jip?"

"Cap'n Wheeler's got him. He's fine."

Joaquin breathed a sigh of relief. He thought of all the hours he and his own dog Solo Vino had spent with the little dog, Jeff Kidder's pride and joy.

He and Shaw continued on down the dusty street. Shaw said, "I mean it, Joaquin. You need to watch your back if these guys are *really* after you." He hesitated. "Cap'n says they'll stop at nothing. He's concerned about you and your family."

"*My family!*" Joaquin stopped again. Suddenly, he couldn't breathe. He reached out grasping Shaw's arms. "My family?" His eyes hardened. "They wouldn't *dare!*"

Shaw didn't respond, but shuffled his boots again. Joaquin released all the air from his lungs, then strode down the street with Shaw catching up. "We've got to catch these guys, Frank."

"Yes, we do," said Shaw emphatically.

They heard shots down the street from where they stood. The Rangers looked at each other. Joaquin said it for both of them, "The Cowboy Home Saloon?"

Shaw nodded. "Yep. What else is new?"

The Rangers had assisted Deputy Constable Shorty Corson in arresting two men disturbing the peace in the saloon the previous evening. The Cowboy Home Saloon was run by Tom Hudspeth and a Texas thug by the name of Lorenzo "Lon" Bass. Bass hated all Rangers—Texan or Arizonan. Rangers were a pain in his backside all his adult life, and he didn't mind displaying his hatred for the lawmen.

The Rangers ran down the dusty street. Joaquin started to step up onto the board sidewalk; he hesitated momentarily as his gaze fell on a distinct marking in the dust near the sidewalk. *A fresh boot print with the outside heel built up on the right side!*

Is Billy Calhoun's murderer here? In the saloon? His heart beating, Joaquin drew his revolver, cocked it as he as stayed low and quickly entered the smoke-filled saloon through the batwing doors. He remembered Elliott's advice. *Don't stand in them doorways long, boy. They're killin' alleys if someone is waitin' on ya.* He moved swiftly to his left, gun leveled as he allowed his eyes to adjust. In his peripheral vision, he saw Shaw step inside to the right of the door. The saloon was packed with male customers, and the usual saloon girls were working the room.

One man to his right caught his attention as he quickly surveyed the room. The man was wearing black clothes and a black hat adorned with silver conchos for a hat band. Then Joaquin's eyes focused on a man who stood alone in the middle of the floor, waving his six-shooter around the room. He let out a loud yell and fired a shot into the ceiling.

Joaquin advanced, flanked by Shaw. He pointed his revolver at the man. "Drop the gun, mister! Arizona Rangers."

The disheveled man dropped his arm to his side, but didn't let go of the six-shooter. He turned to face Joaquin. "Wel-l-l, if it ain't the wet-earred pup." The drunken man's unshaven, sweaty face could barely mouth the words to speak. "Go on, *git.*" Spittle flew from his numb lips. "Lon don't want no greaser lovin' Rangers in here." He belched.

"I said, *drop it.* Now!" Joaquin crouched, supporting his strong hand with his left. He was ten feet from the man now, looking into his eyes. The drunk dropped his gun to the floor as he stared into the hard eyes facing him.

Joaquin heard Shaw yell out to him, "*Watch out*—on your left!"

Turning, he saw Lon Bass near him. *How the hell did he get there?*

Bass's face was ugly. "I'll beat your damn face off ya!" He brought a revolver up and hit Joaquin squarely in the face, smashing his cheek bone. Blood gushed from the wound as Joaquin staggered back, stunned. A gun shot deafened Joaquin. He looked at Bass through the thick smoke-filled room. In slow motion, he saw the owner leveling the revolver at him. Joaquin heard someone hitting the floor near him.

Shaw shouted, "I've been hit. Watch your back!"

Dizzy, reeling from the blow to his cheek, Joaquin pointed quickly at Bass without aiming, pulling the trigger. Bass fired simultaneously. Joaquin felt the hot round sear his neck as it narrowly missed him. Joaquin cocked and fired, hitting Bass in the chest again.

Joaquin dove to his knees near Shaw as he felt two rounds pass near this head, one knocking his hat off. He flattened himself on the saloon floor near Shaw, aiming to fire in the direction the rounds had come from. The batwing doors flopped. The assailant had most likely exited the saloon.

"Are you okay, Frank?"

"They set us up, Joaquin. *My back!* Someone shot me in the back." Blood trickled from Shaw's mouth onto the dirty saloon floor.

"Take it easy, Frank. I'll get you to a doctor." He stood waving his six-shooter at the rowdy crowd. "Stand back! Get back!"

They did as they were told, but one drunken patron yelled, "You killed Lon, you son-of-a-bitch!"

Joaquin shoved men in front of him as he strode up to the man who had just spoken. He shoved his .45 Colt under the man's nose. "Yeah, I killed him. He tried to kill me. Now, *back off!*"

The batwing doors opened suddenly behind Joaquin. He whirled around to see the town's Constable and Deputy Constable barge into the saloon, both carrying shotguns.

Joaquin's thoughts flashed to his family at the ranch. Why would someone harm *them?* For what he had done in the line of duty? He couldn't imagine anyone being so evil or mean. What kind of men were they—this gun running bunch of riffraff? Was the man who shot Shaw in the back the same man who murdered Billy Calhoun? *I've got to get*

Frank to a doctor, get word to Captain Wheeler, and ride hard for the ranch on Cienega Creek. I can't take any chances with my family's lives!

CHAPTER TWENTY-SEVEN

Elliott removed his battered old Stetson and mopped his brow with his shirt sleeve. His white hair shone in the afternoon sunshine; his drooping, white mustache stood out in contrast against his deeply tanned, leathery face. He sauntered over to his Indian pony tied to a small tree along the San Pedro River. Carefully, he lifted the flap on his saddle bags and placed the fencing pliers inside. Turning, he said, "Well, *mi'jo*, I'm plumb wore down to the nub, and it ain't even time to quit work yet."

A tall, thin boy of thirteen going on fourteen leaned against his wooden crutches and smiled at the old Ranger. "Me too, Dad! And I don't work nearly as hard as you."

Elliott returned the smile, removed the canteen from the saddle horn, and walked over to the boy. He pulled the cork on the canteen, offering a drink to Tim Campbell. The boy drank his fill as the old man helped hold the canteen. Then Elliott tipped the canteen, drinking his fill of the cool water. Wiping his lips and mustache, he motioned toward a large cottonwood tree, "Let's go set a spell, Timmy."

They sat for several minutes, enjoying the moment, the out-of-doors, the quietness. A mourning dove cooed in the tree above them, then another spoke from a distant tree near the water's edge. They watched as a red-tailed hawk swooped down along the tree line, looking for prey. Elliott broke the silence, "I shore appreciate your help, Timmy—your company, too."

Tim met the old man's eyes. "I *like* working with you, learning how to do things."

"You're a doggoned good learner, I'd say."

"Thanks," the boy returned.

Elliott looked out over the landscape. "It's a cotton-pickin' shame what with all these fences an' sech."

Timmy said nothing knowing his dad had more to say on the subject. He moved his crutches off to the side and reached into the cotton sack containing lunch for both of them.

The old man sighed heavily. "There was the day, son. Why, this country was *wide* open fer as far as you could see. Warn't no fences atall. Hell, warn't no people to speak of— 'cepting them damned Apaches. Me an' your Granddaddy, we run a herd of cattle through here, and we knowed this was *some* country!" He stopped in his conversation, cocking his head at the boy near his side. "Course you heerd all this ten times over, ain't ya, *mijo?*"

The boy tilted his hat back on his head with his thumb as he had seen Elliott do so often. "I like hearing about the old times."

Elliott smiled, his dark face wrinkling in the sunlight. "You're shore a good 'un, son. I'm proud to be your daddy." He peered at his young companion again, noted the resemblance of his wife Megan in the kind face, the eyes, and the way the boy smiled and held himself. Seeing the blue cotton work shirt and jeans were dusty and soiled, he remarked, "Your Mom ain't gonna be happy with you bein' dirty an' all."

Tim handed Elliott a piece of fried chicken and an apple. "Oh, mom won't care a bit. She likes me to work and spend time with you."

Elliott took a bite out of the chicken leg. "I reckon you're right at thet, *mijo.*"

They ate in silence, the old man and the boy, enjoying being together in the quiet of a good day. Elliott passed the canteen over to the boy, allowed him to drink, then took a big swig of the water himself to wash his lunch down. He noticed the boy looking at the Colt .45 in the shoulder holster under his left arm pit. He was quiet for a time.

"If a man's got something to say ... why, I reckon he ought to jest say it, Timmy."

"I was just wondering—?"

The old Ranger grinned. "You was, was ya?"

"Yes sir. Why you carry your gun with you all the time now." The boy swallowed the last bite of his chicken. "You didn't used to. Not till that bad man showed up at the ranch."

Elliott rubbed the whiskers on his chin, tilted his hat back with his thumb, and reached in his pants pocket for his pocket knife. The boy's face was solemn, frowning. The old Ranger sliced the apple into pieces, handing them to Tim. "Gimme yours, son. You go on an' eat them slices. It'll be a sight easier on your teeth."

Elliott sliced the other apple then stored his knife in his pocket. "Thet man is a badun alright, Timmy. He's worse—a killer—an' he likes it."

"Will he come back here?" the boy asked tentatively.

Elliott swallowed a chewed slice of apple. "I garntee it, *mijo*. When he comes, it'll be with plenty o' help, and it won't be no social call."

"*Why?* We haven't done anything to him, have we?"

"Don't matter, boy. He works fer a man thet ain't exactly happy with me. Another badun, most likely worse in a lot of ways than Coburn."

"What can we do, Dad," Tim asked anxiously.

"I've been thinkin' on thet. A lot lately," replied the old man.

"Why not leave?"

Elliott's voice was hard, "Once you start runnin', you'll always run when times git tight, son. Best to stand an' fight."

Minutes ticked by. Neither of them spoke, their faces grim. Tim pulled his hat back down on his head. "I'm scared ... really scared," he said.

Elliott placed his arm over the boy's shoulder. "No need fer thet, *mijo*. As long as I've got a breath in me, I'd never allow any harm come to you." His piercing blue eyes looked into Tim's eyes. "You know thet, don't you?"

"Yes, sir." The boy attempted a weak smile.

Quiet ensued the moment again, the old man and boy each in deep thought. Birds chirped gaily in the trees along the river bank, flying from tree to tree. It was the boy who spoke. "Elliott, you ever been afraid of dying?"

The old man patted the young boy on the arm. "Shore. Lots o' times. Ever'body gits scared, but when the time comes ... you gotta put the fear aside."

Elliott looked out across the high sacaton grass. "As for dyin'. Why, ever' body has to die, boy." He smiled. "It's the way o' things. Ain't nothin' to be scared about."

"I can't help it," Tim said. "I'm not so afraid for me as Mom and you."

"Wel-l-l, thet's plumb nice o' ya, *mijo*. It figgers you'd think o' others first." Elliott rose to his knees, grimacing at the pain in his right knee. He took the boy in his arms, holding him close. "Timmy, I won't never let you an' your mom down. You're *all* I have in this world. Don't think I take thet lightly, boy."

The boy sobbed, "I love you, Dad."

"I reckon I *know* thet." The old man hugged the boy tightly. Then he released him, patted him on the back and stood up, reaching into the pocket of his pants. He withdrew an old brown rosary. Peering longingly at it, he handed it to the boy.

"Go on, take it, *mijo*. It's yours now."

The boy protested. "No. I can't take your rosary. I know what it means to you." He shook his head, refusing. "I see you use it to pray everyday."

The old man insisted, opening the boy's hand, placing it firmly inside. He smiled, a peace coming over him. "I reckon it's yours now. I want you to have it. You pray ever' day thet you an' your mom stay safe. I've done my share o' prayin'. I reckon I got them prayers memorized by now—don't need no rosary anymore."

"I don't know how—"

Elliott reached down, taking the rosary from the boy. "It's easy, son. If an old cowpuncher with no schoolin' kin learn, it'll be a cinch fer you." He showed Tim which prayer to pray for the cross and then each bead. They went over each prayer several times. Elliott was amazed at how quickly the boy learned.

Standing, Elliott said, "You remember there's shore 'nough a Gawd who's always listenin'; he don't much care if you say the right words—the idée is to ask him fer help in whatever words come to mind."

"Yes sir."

The Indian pony stamped his foot. Elliott reached in his shirt pocket, and withdrew a new watch and peered at it. "Well now, *mijo*, this here handy dandy, brand spankin' new watch says we got to git fer home." He gingerly placed the watch back in his pocket. "Can't be late fer supper. Meg'd have my hide."

***

Elliott reached the edge of the clearing to his ranch. He led the Indian pony with Tim astride. Suddenly, something seemed out of place to him. *What the hell's wrong?* It was too quiet. He stopped, looked around. The little white house, the barn—everything looked the same. But he had a bad feeling in his gut. *What is it?* Glancing down, he saw fresh horse tracks. *How many? Oh, my Gawd.* Quickly, he led the pony back from the edge of the clearing and off to a clump of willows. He looked at the boy.

"Somethin's wrong, Timmy. I've got to see to your mom and Li." He helped Tim off the horse, handed him his crutches and passed the reins to him. "You stay here with Indio, son." He saw the raw fear in the boy's face. He forced a smile. "It's goin' to be all right."

He grasped the .30-.40 Winchester rifle and withdrew it from the scabbard, levering a round in the chamber then released the hammer. "Take this and wait here fer me." With that he was gone, moving swiftly around the edge of the clearing and out of sight from the frightened young boy who loved him.

Elliott skirted the clearing to the west, crossing the river and staying to available cover and concealment. The old weathered .45 Colt was in his right hand, his thumb on the hammer. He crossed the river again and paused behind the barn. *Way too damn quiet.* The fear began in the pit of his stomach. Cautiously, he reached out with his left hand and opened the latch on the back gate. He cocked his revolver, opened the gate just enough to get inside then slipped quickly into the dark interior, staying low and moving to his right while his eyes adjusted to the change in light.

He heard nothing, saw no movement. Quiet. *Maybe it ain't nothin', boss.* Kneeling on his good left knee, he surveyed the barn's interior. *I reckon Megan's right. I need to get me some o' them spectacles—can't see worth a damn no more.* Moving slowly, keeping to the stalls on the east side, he inched forward, willing his old eyes to see as sharply as they had when he was young.

He stopped suddenly, a cry escaping his lips, horror on the old weathered face. Directly in front of him, he saw the limp figure of a man hanging from the barn's rafters. He stood there momentarily, unable to move. *Oh, my Gawd!*

Throwing caution to the wind, he de-cocked the revolver, holstered it in the shoulder holster, and sprang forward to the inert figure hanging in the barn. *Hao Li!* He grasped his friend's legs as he fumbled in his pocket for the knife. He tore it from his pocket but couldn't open it as he held his friend's legs tightly. Finally, he let go of the body, opened the knife, reached high over Hao Li's head and cut the rope. The body dropped heavily on top of him, and both of them fell to the barn floor. *Oh ... Gawd!* He sobbed as he struggled to remove the rope from his friend's neck.

Hao Li was dead, the life strangled from him. Li's tongue protruded from his mouth, his neck was broken. The Chinaman's hands were tied securely behind his back. He was stripped naked, beaten severely over most of his body and shot at least once. His face was almost unrecognizable. Elliott felt bile in his throat and emptied his stomach, retching again and again on all fours.

He straightened. *Megan!* He stood quickly, drawing his revolver and cocking it. Running out of the barn and toward the house, he yelled, "Megan! Megan!" He reached the front steps and started up them when his right knee buckled. Almost falling headlong, he regained his balance, completed the steps and slammed the front door open. *"Megan!"*

His gun covered the interior of the house. *No one!* He moved more cautiously now, the revolver held out in front, turning in unison with his body. The room was in disarray—furniture overturned, broken and smashed lamps, dishes, and other personal items destroyed. The door to the bedroom was ajar. He moved toward it, catlike. The old worn out muscles and sinew moved as they had in his younger days only because he willed it so. His face was hardened, grim as he kicked the door open and stepped inside.

No one. Nothing. But wait. *What's this on the bed?* Elliott reached down and picked up a piece of paper. He held it in the light out at arm's length. A scrawled note read: "Wouldn't listen. Boss don't like to wait. Your woman and the crippled boy are next. The chink fought hard till I shot him in the gut."

Elliott wadded the paper up in his fist and threw it to the floor. He stood there, not moving, numb and helpless. Finally, he de-cocked the six-shooter, turned and started out of the bedroom. *Where's Meg?*

He heard a horse coming into the ranch yard at a run. He ran to the front door and peered out. It was Megan, and she was leading the Indian pony with Tim astride hanging onto the saddle horn with his left hand, his right holding the rifle. *Thank God, she's all right.*

The old Ranger stepped out onto the porch, holstering the .45 Colt. Megan Campbell slid off the horse and ran to him as he stepped off the porch. She saw his face. "What happened, Elliott?" she asked breathlessly. "I went over to St. David this morning to visit my friend Sally."

"Don't go in the barn or let the boy neither, Meg."

A frown formed on her face. She repeated the question with more urgency, "What happened?"

Elliott held her tightly before he spoke. "Li's dead, Meg. They've killed him." He swallowed hard. "They ... hung him in the barn."

"*What?*" She pulled back from him, looking into the icy, blue eyes and knew he spoke the truth. "Oh, my God. *My God* ... who ... who would do such a thing?"

"I reckon its Hyde's bunch o' no good sumbitches."

"But why would they do such a thing to Li, Elliott. *Why?*" She sobbed.

Elliott held her tightly, his face grim as he looked at the boy still astride the Indian pony. *What do I say to Timmy? Why do men do such terrible things? Because others are different from them?* It would be dark soon; he needed to take care of Hao Li—cover him. Then he'd carry him up the hill and bury him next to his first wife and son. A rare tear trickled down the tanned leathery face then another. He sighed deeply, the tears stopped as suddenly as they had begun.

His voice had a metallic ring to it, "You an' Timmy go on into the house, Meg. I'll tend to my good friend."

CHAPTER TWENTY-EIGHT
Winter, 1909

From the hilltop behind the cover of small oak trees, Fernando stood beside the bay horse whose tail constantly swished. His dark brown face was pensive, frowning at times as he watched the small band of horsemen in the arroyo below. Who were these heavily armed men? If he were in Mexico, he would know them to be bandits, but here? Maybe they were lawmen? No, he thought not. Even at this distance, he knew they were bad men.

He swallowed with difficulty, fear growing in his stomach. Squinting his eyes to see better, he observed six horsemen, several were wearing *bandoleros* loaded with ammunition, all carried rifles in their scabbards, and pistols on their belts. Three of the men wore wide sombreros like his. *Mexicanos?* They were traveling northwest toward the Cienega Ranch headquarters. Why? There were no towns or other ranches in the vicinity. What could they possibly want at the ranch?

Fernando took off his sombrero, ran fingers through his coal black hair, then replaced it firmly on his head. He turned, looked at the rifle scabbard carrying the Winchester on his saddle. He could ride down and confront them—ask what their intentions were. He rubbed his jaw, thinking. No. He was a *Mexicano* who spoke very little English. They would just shoot him and be on their way. No one would ever miss him or care that he was dead.

Ayadame, Dios. He felt himself sweating the more

he thought of the situation. Then he heard a little voice telling him, "Leave, Fernando. Leave now!" He had been thinking of returning home to Sonora, Mexico of late to his *esposa* and *niña*. His family was everything to him, and he missed them terribly. Why not just go home? He could send the Campbells the money for the horse, saddle, and rifle. He had saved his money for nearly a year, and he had it with him. He always carried it with him in the money belt around his slender waist.

The bay gelding startled him by suddenly shaking his bridle. Fernando swallowed hard again. "*Vayase, 'horita,*" the little voice said to him again. Just leave, without saying goodbye to the very people who had been so kind to him? Leave them without any warning as to the bad men down in the arroyo? He shook his head. Those men were most likely just passing through the countryside and didn't even know the whereabouts of the Cienega Ranch. He owed the Campbells nothing.

He had his own family to think of now. Looking up at the clear, blue sky, he thought he saw an image of his daughter, and he smiled. He thought he felt her tugging at his trousers as she smiled shyly back at him. Her black, curly hair shone in the sunlight. *Mi'ja, te amo*, he whispered his love to her.

Fernando led the bay down behind the hill, the large rowels of his spurs jingling musically, much to his chagrin. His face grim, he walked the horse along a small arroyo, using the cover of the drainage and occasional oak trees. As he mounted, he felt perspiration on his cotton work shirt between the shoulder blades. It was a cool day.

***

Carmen Ponce stood on the porch of the old ranch house and shook the rug. Then she shook it again, harder this time. She gazed at the sky—maybe another hour before dark. She had promised to help Marian Campbell fix supper tonight for everyone to eat together. As she turned to re-enter the ranch house, she heard a horse coming in fast from the south. Carmen frowned as she turned toward the horse and rider.

Fernando's bay slid to a stop in front of the ranch house. He swung down quickly, dropped the reins to the ground, and ran toward her. She looked at the ground-tied bay all lathered up, wheezing as it stood trembling.

"Fernando! What do you think you're doing to that horse?" she shouted in Spanish.

He leaped up on the porch, his eyes fierce. "Bad men ... coming, *Señora!*"

"*Bad men?* Whatever on earth are you *talking* about?" she exclaimed, dropping the rug.

"*Where is el chiquito?*" he rasped.

Carmen stepped back away from the dark, young man. She had never seen him like this; it frightened her.

Fernando reached out and grasped her shoulders roughly. "*Where is Lou?*"

She looked into his fierce eyes, but said nothing. He moved her aside, entered the open door and rushed inside shouting, "Lou! Lou! *Venga aquí!*"

A tentative soft voice responded, "Nan-do?"

Fernando turned, seeing the little boy behind the door. He reached down, scooped him into his arms.

Carmen's hard voice said, "You *put* him down. Now!" She held a .45 Colt that was leveled at him.

He held the boy more tightly. "*Oigame, Señora.* We have no time for this. The bad men are only minutes behind me. We must act now." He shifted the boy in his arms. "Where is Marion ... Domingo?"

The realization of what the Mexican said finally sank into her rattled brain. "They're at the main ranch house waiting for us to eat supper together." She lowered the revolver.

"Take Lou there now."

She hesitated, started to say something but could not formulate a sentence.

"Please. Do it now."

Fernando turned, racing back out to the bay. He pulled the rifle from the scabbard, then jerked the saddle and bridle from him, slapping him on the rump. The tired horse trotted away from the house toward Cienega Creek.

They ran toward the main ranch house together, the little boy falling several times. Fernando gave the rifle to Carmen, picked Lou up and ran as fast as he could to the house. Carmen was there ahead of him, the old rough-hewn door open for him to bolt through.

***

Fernando stood inside near the window. He felt both hands sweating as the riders rode into the Cienga ranch headquarters—six of them, all heavily armed. Their purpose seemed clear enough as they did not stop at Carmen's *casita*. Instead they rode directly to the main house. Their leader stepped down from his horse. He had a large sweat-stained gray sombrero, a dark swarthy complexion and a dirty, unshaven face. Wearing a leather *bandolero* bristling with heavy rifle bullets and two belt pistols, he looked confident of the easy task ahead of him.

Gray-haired Marion Campbell stood near an open window armed with a .30-.40 1895 Winchester. Her wrinkled face was hardened. On the other side, Carmen's father Domingo stood near an open window armed with an old 1873 Winchester rifle. Near the rear door, Carmen knelt grasping a .45 Colt revolver. Her son Lou sat behind her, his face displaying dismay and uncertainty of what was unfolding before them.

"Hell-o de house?" the bandit called out. The other men sat in their saddles chuckling.

Fernando opened the old rough, wooden door and stepped out onto the porch holding the Winchester tightly. His voice quavered as he spoke, *"¿Qué quieren?"*

The hardened bandit leader looked at the young inexperienced Mexican. He grinned broadly, the gold tooth in the front of his mouth presenting itself boldly. "What do *I* want?" He laughed. Pointing a finger at Fernando, he continued harshly, "I wish to *speek* with *Señor* Joaquin Campbell." His hands were now on both pistols at his side.

"*Señor* Campbell is not here," returned Fernando. He knew the raw fear showed in his voice, but he could not control it. His legs trembled. *Our Father who art in heaven ...*

"*Valgame.*" The swarthy face was not smiling. "My *jefe, Señor* Hyde, he wishes for me to geeve heem—yew—something," he said in English.

The bandit feigned looking back toward the men behind him. As he turned, he swiftly drew both six-shooters. Fernando had no time to think. He pulled the rifle stock to his cheek and fired, striking the man directly in the center of his chest, knocking him back off the porch.

A moment of hesitation, then the quiet was shattered as Fernando shot the next closest man. He saw the man drop his pistol and slump forward before falling off his horse to the ground. Fernando levered a round into the chamber and shot another bandit off his horse. The bandit screamed, his foot caught in the stirrup. Shots were fired from inside the house. Horses reared, ran away in all directions. Men cursed in Spanish and English.

Frightened, Fernando heard bullets hit the house and porch near him, splintering wood. Hot rounds passed close to him. He could not move but kept firing. He felt the hammer click on an empty chamber. Kneeling, he reached in his shirt pocket for the extra shells. The bandits were caught out in the open in front of the house. They had nowhere to go for cover. Only one was left standing. He yelled obscenities in Spanish as he charged the porch, shooting as he came. Fernando felt the searing bullet enter his chest. Then another, low down near his ribs on the right side. He fell back, dropping the rifle.

A shotgun fired near him, cutting the bandit nearly in two at the bottom of porch. Fernando lay on his side, his brown face now pale. The intense pain in his chest and side burned uncontrollably.

The shooting stopped. An eerie stillness settled over the scene. A bandit cried out another obscenity in Spanish; a resounding pistol shot silenced it. Fernando was numb, then cold. He thought of what he had done. *God, please forgive me for taking these men's lives.*

Then he thought of his family, far away in Mexico. A tear trickled down his cheek. He saw his wife, his little daughter. They were smiling, holding his hands. "We are proud of you, Fernando. You stood and fought when it was right to do so, when others would have run away," his wife said to him in English. Their images faded away.

Strong hands touched him. "Fernando, it's me, Joaquin."

Fernando opened his eyes and saw the young Ranger leaning over him. He tried to smile, wincing with pain. He felt a dog lick his hand. *Solo Vino.*

"I'm going to carry you inside." Joaquin's voice cracked in mid-sentence.

Summoning all his strength, Fernando stammered, "No. No, *jefe*. Hurts ... too much ... please."

A small hand touched his cheek, warming him. "Nan-do?"

Fernando struggled to speak. "Lou ... *mijo ...como*

estas?"

Joaquin answered, "He's fine. Everyone is fine, thanks to you, my friend."

A smile formed on the Mexican's face. A groan escaped his mouth; he settled back quietly on the porch. His face peaceful, the white pallor faded with the brown color returning.

CHAPTER TWENTY-NINE

Tim Campbell supported himself with one wooden crutch as he opened the door to Elliott's ranch house with the other crutch. He stepped out onto the porch, the screen door closing behind him. A cow bellowed in the distance then the milk cow from the barn. Supporting himself upright with both crutches, he looked out over the southwestern horizon and stared at the sky. His mouth flew open. The sunrise was a *bright* red, almost blood-red. In all his youthful years, he had never seen the sky so red—so bright red. It was indescribable—beautiful, magnificent, awesome, and ominous all at the same time.

Breathlessly, he sat in Elliott's rocking chair, watching the unusual sunrise fade in the eastern skies. He saw Elliott come from the barn, carrying a milk pail. As the old Ranger reached the porch, a man on horseback appeared in the clearing. Without speaking, Tim pointed toward the approaching horseman. Elliott quickly set the pail of milk on the porch and turned, facing the oncoming intruder with his hand on the old .45 Colt revolver in the leather shoulder holster under his left armpit.

Tim watched Elliott's piercing blue eyes scan the horizon. No one else appeared. The man rode up to within a dozen yards. The white whiskers on the leathery, dark brown face betrayed his age and ethnicity. He wore a large sombrero and dusty range clothes. Armed with a belt pistol, his hands on the saddle horn, he leaned forward in the saddle peering at Elliott. Neither of the men spoke, but stared at each other.

The Mexican smiled, his face wrinkling. "Elliott, you ol' son-of-a-beech."

Elliott removed his hand from the gun butt, and returned the smile. "Rudolpho, *mi amigo.* Get down off thet hoss; come in and git somethin' to eat."

The old Mexican sat his horse, the smile faded. *"Gracias, hombre."* He flicked the reins in his left hand impatiently. "There are men coming—soon—right behind me." He paused. "They have orders to kill you." He motioned toward Tim Campbell sitting on the porch. "To kill *all* of you, to the last man."

"Why are you telling me this, Rudy?"

The old man sighed as he straightened himself in the saddle. "Damned if I know. You saved my life once. I owe you and—"

Elliott's face was tight. "And—?"

"I've killed many men in my life, and like you, my friend, I will be judged by God some day." He shrugged. "But I have *never* killed a woman or a boy."

"My thanks to you, old friend. You'd best ride hard."

The old Mexican lithely swung his right leg over the saddle horn, and slid to the ground. "Reckon I'll stay."

"You don't owe me *thet* much."

Rudolpho turned toward the barn, leading his horse. "I put the horse out of sight, and then I'll need a shotgun." His eyes twinkled as he smiled proudly showing a full head of teeth. "I do my best work with the *escopeta. ¿Recuerda, amigo?"*

"How many, Rudy? Who's leading 'em?" asked Elliott.

The old Mexican said over his shoulder, "Twelve of the best men Hyde's got, and a *caca caliente* by the name of

Coburn is running things." He shook his head. "*Cabrones—todos.*"

"This Coburn ... he wears a black hat with silver conchos for a hat band?"

"*Sí, viejito,*" replied Rudolpho.

***

Megan's tense face was chalk-white. She stood listening to Elliott, wringing her hands.

"Meg, you got to go fer help. There's no other way. We can't hold this many fer too long," he implored her.

"*No!* I won't leave you and Timmy. That's final."

Grasping her shoulders, he said softly, "It's the only way, Meg." He let go of her, shaking his head. "If you don't make it ..." He let the words sink in. "... we're all dead, I reckon."

"But, surely there's another way?" she asked.

His piercing blue eyes looked into the beautiful brown eyes of his wife. "No. No, Meg—there ain't. I'm sorry; I didn't see this comin' so soon."

Her face softened. "It's not your fault, Elliott."

The old Mexican called out from the front of the house. "They're startin' to encircle the place. She needs to *move! Now, dammit!*"

Elliott gave her a .45 Colt revolver, removed the skinning knife from the leather sheath attached to his pistol belt and handed it to her. "Take these. *Go!*" He hugged her tightly.

"I never met a woman quite like you, Megan. Gawd's been awful good to me. I can never repay you fer lovin' me."

He held her out at arm's length. "Git to St. David—to Sally's house. Use their telephone—call fer the Deputy Sheriff stationed there and the Ranger office down in Naco."

"My Timmy?" she cried out holding the boy tightly

next to her.

"I give ya my word, Meg. No harm'll come to the boy."

She did not move, tears streaming down her face.

"Meg. *Listen to me.* Timmy can't git past them men with his crutches. Maybe even you can't. You're the best chance we got o' makin' it through."

The Mexican intervened again. "She needs to go *now!*"

Elliott hugged her tight, kissed her, smelling her hair, breathing in her very essence. He pushed her to the rear door. "You remember what I told ya?"

"Yes," she barely whispered.

"Wait for the diversion from the front then move fast!"

He turned abruptly moving to the front open window. He knelt down gingerly, feeling the pain shooting up into his right knee. Picking up the .30-.40 Winchester rifle, he peered out to the clearing. He flipped the adjustable sights up into position. With both eyes open, he looked through the sights, focusing on a man horseback, somewhat concealed in the outlying vegetation of the riparian area. He saw the man's shoulder come into view as he addressed Rudolpho. "On the count o' three, Rudy."

"*Sí, compadre.*"

At the designated count, both rifles thundered simultaneously within the confines of the small ranch house. Two bandits were knocked out of their saddles. Quiet ensued for several moments, and then men shouted curses and orders and fired into the front of the house. Elliott lay flat on the floor as bullets slammed through the windows and into the wooden structure, tearing into the interior of the small house. He knew Timmy was safe behind the big iron cook stove, armed with Rudolpho's .45 Colt. Turning, he looked at the back door. Megan was gone.

CHAPTER THIRTY

Tears streaming down her face, Megan Campbell ran out the back door clutching the six-shooter and skinning knife in either hand. She reached the outhouse without incident. Breathing hard, she peered toward the large cottonwood tree about thirty yards away. Elliott told her there would most likely be someone there to monitor their back door. Sporadic shooting continued from the front of the little ranch house. She heard someone screaming orders in the midst of all the firing.

Placing the weapons behind her skirt, she took a deep breath, stepped out from behind the outhouse, and headed for the big tree. Her heart raced. She tried not to stumble as she walked swiftly toward the cover of the tree and the only way out from this terrible violence. *Please God, help me do this! I don't think I can kill ... even now.* She reached the tree. No one! She licked dry lips and swallowed hard, then looked about as she crouched behind the tree. Still she saw no one. Leaning back she closed her eyes. *Oh, thank you, God! Thank you.*

Her heart still pounded within her chest. *I must go. Now. Every second counts.* She heard more shooting from the house, more screaming, sporadic firing. She opened her eyes as she pushed off the tree. Her eyes stared in terror and paralizing fright. A bandit stood in front of her about ten paces away. Pointing a large six-shooter directly at her, he grinned. "Well now, what have we *here?*"

Megan froze, unable to move her legs. She kept the

knife and gun hidden behind her full skirt. The man walked slowly toward her, his gun still leveled at her, cocked and ready to fire. She backed away from him as he advanced. Tobacco juice stained his mouth and unshaven chin. He flipped his hat off his head, the chin strap securing it around his neck. His clothing was dirty and ragged, the leather riding chaps and boots dusty.

Megan hit the tree hard with her back. She gasped loudly. No where to go, she looked furtively from side to side trying to use only her peripheral vision as she watched the armed man advance. She clutched the knife and pistol in her sweaty palms.

The bandit stopped directly in front of her and roughly shoved the six-shooter under her chin, tilting it upward. Wild-eyed, he cocked his head sideways as he looked her up and down, licking his dried cracked lips.

Megan's heart raced to unbearable limits. Wanting to run, she could not. Instinctively, she knew even if she did, she would be shot dead. These men were killers—bad men who committed ugly atrocities undoubtedly on a frequent basis.

He leaned forward smelling her hair, the gun dropped to his side as he jeered, "Skeered, ain't ya?" He laughed loudly, then said between clenched teeth, "The boss said to kill anybody what come out." Grinning, he looked her up and down again. "But he didn't say nothing' 'bout takin' my time, uh?"

Megan realized he saw the raw fear in her eyes, and he enjoyed it. She was easy prey for the taking. De-cocking and holstering the pistol, he grabbed her shoulders roughly. She knew at that moment he intended to force himself on her, then kill her. Her life was nothing to him.

Fear turned to rage. She heard Elliott's voice, *if one man tries to stop you in close, use the knife. Don't draw attention.*

She dropped the heavy pistol from her trembling left hand. Summoning all her strength, she drove the skinning knife into the bandit's mid-section. *Drive it in hard, Meg, an' up toward his heart.* The bandit screamed. Megan clenched her teeth, grunting as she thrust the blade upward. A groan escaped the man's mouth as he tried to grab at her hands, to somehow dislodge the sharp knife blade. Surprise showed in his eyes, then emptiness. He attempted to yell out for help.

Megan withdrew the bloody knife, grasped the man by his dirty matted hair, and jerked his head back with all her strength. With a rage-filled gasp, she brought the sharp skinning knife under his chin, swiping it as hard and as quickly as she could from right to left. Blood erupted from his throat onto to her face, her clothes. His scream for help was literally cut short as he slumped to the ground, gurgling. She dropped the knife in horror at what she had done.

Leaning back hard against the tree for support, Megan struggled to breathe. She wiped her face. Something obscured her vision. Her hands were soaked in the man's blood. She wiped her face again. Her head pounded as her adrenalin-laden body screamed out to her. Her chest felt as though her heart would explode. *The pistol!* She searched frantically for the six-shooter Elliott had given her. *There it is!* The .45 Colt revolver was partially covered by ground litter and duff. She picked it up and started to run, pausing to think. *Wait!* She returned to the dead bandit and retrieved his six-shooter.

His horse can't be too far. Oh, my God. What have I done? She searched the immediate area, found nothing, and turned to go when she spied the sorrel tied to a small cottonwood tree some distance to the south of her location. She ran to the horse, untied him. Looking all around, she saw no one else in her vicinity. The shooting at the ranch house had subsided. Megan took one last look to ensure no one else had seen her and shoved the extra pistol in the man's bedroll behind the saddle. Her blood-stained face was held high, the brown eyes hardened as she grabbed the horn with her right hand, the horse's mane near the withers with her left hand and vaulted into the saddle, her skirt flying up into the air as she mounted.

Digging her heels into the horse's flanks, she reined him south toward the small Mormon settlement of St. David. She rode him hard, trotting, loping, but never walking. She peered over her shoulder occasionally, the loaded pistol in her right fist. She prayed for the safety of those left behind. *Hail Mary full of grace, the Lord is with thee ...*

CHAPTER THIRTY-ONE

lliott crawled along the litter-strewn floor toward the old iron cook stove. He pulled himself up alongside Tim, who sat behind it with his legs curled up. He pulled himself up alongside. "You okay, *mi'jo?*" he rasped.

Wide-eyed, the boy only nodded his head.

Elliott surveyed him from head to toe, ensuring he was indeed okay. It was his turn to nod his head. Biting his lower lip, he muttered, "I reckon your Mom got plumb away." He sighed deeply and swallowed hard. "She'll be back directly with help, son. I garntee it."

The boy managed a half-smile at the old Ranger then frowned. He dropped the heavy revolver to the floor. "Elliott, you're hurt!" he exclaimed.

"Naw ... I ain't."

Tim reached out to Elliott's blood-soaked shirt near his shoulder and chest, and then he saw the bloody bullet hole in his pants above the knee on his right leg. "Oh, Elliott, they've hurt you."

"They ain't nothin' but scratches, boy." He looked down at the leg. "Hell, thet leg's been nothin' but trouble fer me since I got my knee shot up in Cuba some years back."

He placed his arm around the boy's shoulders and gave him a hug. The boy hugged him back. "Will they come at us again?" Tim asked.

"Yessir, I reckon so," drawled Elliott, sighing again. "They won't come in the daylight. Lost too many men tryin' thet." He leaned his tired head back against the wall. "They'll give us ever'thing they got come nightfall, Timmy."

They sat in silence next to each other, the young boy and the old man, enjoying each other's company and the quiet as they always had done. It was the boy who broke the silence. "Will we live through this?" Tim's voice quavered.

The old man didn't answer right away. Then he said, "I promised yer Mom I wouldn't let 'em hurt you, Timmy." Grinning, he said, "And I ain't never broke my word ... to anybody."

The boy looked at the man he had come to love deeply. Neither said anything for awhile. The Mexican spoke out from the front of the house. "Hey, *hombre*. You got any whiskey for this old *Mexicano? Tengo sed, amigo.*"

Elliott laughed out loud, his body shaking then he coughed violently several times. He wiped at his mouth, and Tim saw blood on his hand and mouth.

"Naw. I ain't got any whiskey in the house, Rudy. When we kill them sumbitches outside, we'll take theirs, uh?"

Rudolpho laughed loudly. "*Si, amigo.* Just like we done in the old days."

Tim whispered, "Elliott, I don't want you to die."

The old Ranger withdrew his arm from around the boy's shoulder and leaned forward. Wincing, he said, "If it's my time to go, *mi'jo*, I reckon I'm ready." He pursed his dry lips then licked at them. "Ya see, son. I've led a mighty rough life over the years. Killed too many men. Done things I ain't proud of. Lived by the sword so to speak."

His tanned, leathery face wrinkled with a grim smile. "You know what they say: live by the sword, die by the sword."

"But ... Elliott, I —"

"I made my peace with God long ago. There's no fear o' dyin' on my part." He reached out and touched his son's face. "You remember, *mijo*, no matter what, I'll *always* be with you an' yer Mom." He tousled the boy hair. His blue eyes shone brightly. "Always."

Tears flowed down the young boy's face. "Yes sir," was all he managed to say.

***

Elliott sat against the braced wooden chair in the middle of the small ranch house. Opening the loading gate of the .45 Colt, he cocked the hammer back, checked if the cylinders were loaded. Smiling to himself, he took a cartridge from his pistol belt and loaded it in the sixth cylinder.

Peering at the old six-shooter in his blood-stained hand, the "M y J" inscription stood out on the worn, brown butt. Maria and Joaquin. How he still loved both of them. His first wife and son. Murdered by Apaches at this same location. When was thet—1872? So many years ago. Time passes way too doggoned fast in life. He had buried them up on the small hill near the house. His old friend Hao Li was alongside them now. *Gawd, how many more will die today? I just wanted to be left alone. To live out my life with Meg and Timmy. No more killin'. Why? Why all this death? Why now?* Chrissake, he was an old man. The Old West as he knew it was a distant image in the horizon. Not real and impossible to get to. Kinda like one o' them mirages he'd heard about.

He shoved the fully loaded pistol back in the worn holster at his side and reached for the one in his shoulder holster. Loading it as he had done with the .45 at his side, he leaned over and grasped the double barrel shotgun. Suddenly, coughing racked his body. He saw more blood on his blue work shirt.

Breaking open the shotgun, he placed "OO" shells

in the chambers, closed it and laid it across his knees. He peered out the side window from his vantage point. Dusk was pert near finished for the day. *Day's damn near all in ... jest like you, hoss.*

Night would be on them soon. Darkness and the final rush from the bandits he expected. He and Rudolpho would be greatly outnumbered. He figured he and his friend had killed four, maybe a half dozen, if they had been lucky in their selected rifle shots. The bandits had been overconfident and paid for it. He positioned the old Mexican near the front door, himself about mid-way to the back door, and the boy behind the wood cook stove. *Gawd, you gotta help me protect Timmy. I warn't here when the Apaches come an' killed my other boy, but keep me alive long 'nough to kill any sumbitch comin' in here to harm Timmy.*

He was racked with a coughing fit again, spitting blood out of his mouth onto the wooden floor. The old Mexican spoke, "Hey, *hombre*, my eyes don't see so good, but my senses tell me, *que por all' vienen.*

"*Yo creo que si,*" said Elliott as he picked up the shotgun, cocking both barrels.

They came at them as he knew they would, as he would have done. As he had done many years before when he hired out his gun. One man feinted at charging the front door, then dropped back into the cover of darkness. But he didn't fool the old Mexican. Rudolpho turned his rifle slightly to his right at a side window, firing two rounds as quick as he could lever another shell into the chamber of the rifle. A loud scream was followed by multiple shots into the house from the front. The shots seemed to search out various locations within the interior.

Then spaced, calculated shots came from both sides, again searching out targets in the dark interior. The old Mexican cried out sharply, cursing the attackers in

Spanish. Elliott felt a tug at his right boot, another hard tug at his shirt near his ribs on the right side. *Be silent, Rudolpho. They want you to tell 'em where you are. Make 'em come on in here.*

Silence again. Elliott waited even as his muscles cried out for him to move. He remembered his father telling him years ago, *patience and wisdom are real virtues, boy.* He laughed to himself at the vision of his dog at home in Texas when he was a kid. He had watched the old dog patiently wait to eat food thrown to him as a skunk intervened and began to eat first.

His skin prickled. They were close. No sound. He listened intently, hardly allowing himself to breathe. Nothing. But he knew when to act. He brought the shotgun up to his shoulder and fired into the window facing him. A man screamed. Elliott rolled to his left as bullets slammed into the back of the chair he had rested against just a second earlier. He aimed the shotgun at the window behind him and fired the second shotgun round, drawing a second scream as a response.

Rudolpho was shooting his rifle rapidly near the front of the house and moving as return fire concentrated on his former position. Elliott lay on his belly, his .45 Colt in his fist. His vision now covered the front and east sides of the house. He waited, feeling pain in his right shoulder and leg. Suddenly, he heard the roar of a six-shooter near the front door and saw the flame erupting from the barrel. The old Mexican cried out and fell to the floor with a thud. Another roar and flame belched from a gun to the right.

Elliott visualized the locations and fired at the first shooter, then snapped a quick shot at the second as he rolled on the floor to his right. Other guns boomed, bullets thudded into the wooden floor where he had been. They followed him as he rolled on the hard floor toward the back of the house. He winced as he felt a round hit him solidly

in the back. It took the breath out of him. The firing continued. He lay on his back, and fanned the hammer of his
six-shooter as he aimed at the muzzle flashes from outside
the windows. The resounding screams made his grim, tired
face smile. *Come an' git it, boys! This ol' man ain't dead by a damn
sight.*

Dropping the empty six-shooter, he drew the .45
Colt from the shoulder holster under his left armpit. Cocking it, he waited. How close am I to Timmy? Dead silence
again. He wanted so badly to call out to the boy to see if he
was all right, but he knew it would draw fire. Suppressing
the urge to cough, he lay on the hard floor, choking in his
own blood. Leaning his head sideways, he spit oozing blood
out of his mouth then allowed gravity to ease the flow of
blood down onto the floor.

They would come in from the rear of the house.
And they would shoot from the side windows—that is if
there were enough of them left. The final entry would be
made from the back to finish him off. Maybe from the front
as well? They probably figured the old Mexican was dead by
now. *You'll be the last in, Coburn, you sumbitch, but I'll still kill ya.*

Elliott's body racked with pain, and the need to
cough violently increased with a burning intensity. But he
waited silently, feeling woozy, dizzy. He heard a slight scrap-
ing sound near the back door. The old Ranger's worried
face smiled. *That's it, boys.* He swallowed blood. It almost
made him choke and cough out in the night. In his best
Texas accent, he thought, *Y'all come on in, ya heah.*

Suddenly, the rear door was kicked in, wood splin-
ters flying into the room, followed by intense gun fire.
Smoke and flame belched from a revolver as a man lurched
into the room, firing as he came. Elliott felt the impact of
bullets hitting him and thudding into the floor near where
he lay. Taking his time, he shot at the man, just above the

muzzle flashes. The shooting stopped. The man stumbled in the doorway, gasping.

With great effort, Elliott pulled himself up to his knees, fanning the hammer of his six-shooter. The bandit fell backward out of the doorway as the heavy slugs hit him hard. Elliott teetered on his knees, feeling weak and sick to his stomach. He coughed violently, almost fainting. Silence again. Struggling to maintain his senses, he strained to hear something, anything. Nothing. *Maybe Coburn ran?* No. No gunman worth his salt would do that.

Elliott slumped back onto his heels. A wave of nausea overcame him, and he vomited onto the floor. His ears, his head pounded unrelentingly. He thought he heard something. What was it? *Yes!* The cocking of a revolver then another! But where? Then he knew, whirling around to face the front of the house. The .45 slug hit him in his left side, knocking him back onto the floor. He lost his grip on the six-shooter.

He heard the gunman step forward then kick his gun. It skittered along the wooden floor away from him. Elliott's eyes searched out the dark room for the gunman. A small amount of ambient light reflected off the silver conchos adorning the black hat.

"Coburn?"

A chuckle. "You got any hide-away guns, Elliott?"

"If I did, you'd be dead."

Another chuckle. Coburn walked up to him, standing over him. He holstered one pistol. He reached in his vest pocket as he kept the old Ranger covered with the other pistol. "You tough ol' *bastard*, I'm the only one left standing."

Elliott did not reply.

Coburn asked, "Who was the other one, near the front?"

Elliott coughed violently, blood spilling out onto his mouth and chin. "Rudolpho."

Grunting, Coburn brought a match up sharply along his pant leg. Once lit, it brought the room some much needed light. "I just wanted to see your face when I kill you." He grinned as he pointed his six-shooter at Elliott.

A soft voice spoke near the kitchen stove, "Drop the gun, mister. I don't want to shoot you."

Coburn lifted the burning wooden match up higher and saw Tim Campbell sitting behind the stove. He laughed out loud then blew the match out. "*You* drop your gun, boy. Maybe I won't kill you, uh?"

Tim's voice quavered as he held the heavy .45 Colt with both hands, "I mean it, mister."

"You don't have the guts to shoot me, boy. And what's more, you can't hit me from that distance even if you wanted to," replied Coburn. He swung his gun up toward the boy.

A shot rang out from behind Elliott. The back of Coburn's head exploded. Still, he stood, not dropping his gun. Tim scrambled forward and rose to his knees. He fanned the hammer of the .45 Colt with the palm of his left hand. The big revolver thundered time and time again until the hammer clicked on an empty chamber. He knelt there for some time then threw the empty gun at the killer lying crumpled on the floor.

It was then he saw one of the killer's boot heels had the outside edge built up.

Crawling over on the floor, he knelt by the old Ranger. "*Elliott?*"

"I'm fit as a fiddle, *mijo*," rasped Elliott. He reached out grasping the boy's hand. Concern showed in his voice. "You okay, boy? You ain't hurt none, are ya?"

The boy moved closer. "I'm fine."

The old Ranger relaxed, and squeezed Tim's hand. "I'm real proud o' ya, Timmy." A rack of coughing interrupted him then he continued, "A father couldn't ... ask fer a better son ... a better friend, than you ... Timmy, boy." He smiled. "Look to our friend Rudy, will ya?"

Tears streamed down the boy's face. "Yes sir."

Light was breaking in the eastern skies. Elliott heard the boy crawling toward the front of the house. As he lay on the hard floor, he closed his eyes. *I'll just take me a little nap then git up an' help Timmy. It was so quiet. He thought of his Megan. Gawd, I shore love her.* He was tired. He wanted to sleep.

Elliott heard horses out in front of the house. He heard Megan yelling for him, for Timmy. Men's voices. The voices were muted. *Can't hear a damn thing anymore.*

His haggard face broke into a smile as he saw images of his first wife and son. She walked toward him carrying their son, reaching out to him. He had seen the image before but now ... he knew it was time, and it was okay. This time he meant it when he said, "Let's go home, Maria."

CHAPTER THIRTY-TWO
February 1, 1909

With Captain Harry Wheeler at the helm, the Rangers rode hard through the night. Every last man of them, minus Jeff Kidder. Their purpose was clear and their grim faces displayed hardness as well as a set determination in completing their new mission. It was personal now, and they all knew it. They rode in a column of twos. Joaquin Campbell rode his paint horse directly behind Wheeler. Chapo Carter rode next to him, followed by Frank Shaw, who had recovered fully from injuries sustained in the Douglas ambush. Oliver Palmer rode next to him. Nineteen strong—not so many, but Arizona Territory's best.

Dawn broke over the southwestern horizon as they rode across the border into Naco, Mexico. A group of twenty horsemen waited for them in the still, cold morning. Joaquin saw a grinning Colonel Kosterlitzky of the Mexican Rurales astride his white gelding.

He spoke to Wheeler, *"Bueños días, Capitan!"* A large pointed sombrero sat atop his head. The Russian-turned-Mexican wore the gray uniform of the Rurales as did his men accompanying him. The Rurales worked directly for *El Presidente*, the President of Mexico, and answered to no one else. Ruthless and fearless, they were selected to remove Mexico of banditry and had accomplished the task for the most part. But they were hated by some for their unsavory tactics and alleged atrocities.

Wheeler leaned forward in the saddle, his palms on the saddle horn. *"Bueños días, Emilio."*

"Welcome to *Mexico*, my law enforcement friends." Kosterlitzky stretched in his saddle, breathing in the early morning fresh air. He peered across at Wheeler, and then looked at the Rangers grouped behind their captain. "I see you are ready for the task ahead of us."

"We are more than ready," replied Wheeler grimly.

A smile toyed at the Colonel's mouth. *"Señor* Hyde's hacienda is but a few miles from here." He played with his black mustache, pulling at the ends. "I have two questions for you, Captain Wheeler, before we depart."

"What is it?" retorted Wheeler.

"These bandits—these *cabrones*—have killed two of your Rangers and my friend, Elliott, yes?"

"Yes. And they continue to run guns across the border."

"Ah, yes." Kosterlitzky pulled at the mustache again. "And you are prepared to do what, *Capitan?"*

Joaquin saw a glint in the colonel's eyes, a hardness in his face as he looked across at Wheeler.

Harry Wheeler said, "I am prepared to end this menace to Mexico and the Territory of Arizona, here and now. We will capture all these bandits, meet them with deadly force, if necessary, to accomplish this task."

"I must remind you, *Capitan,* that you are in Mexico. And as such, *I* am in charge. You will comply with my wishes and those of my *Presidente."*

"Of course, Emilio," replied Wheeler. "I plan to file extradition papers for Hyde and any others captured who are implicated in the murders of American citizens."

Kosterlitzky rubbed his clean-shaven jaw. "He is wanted for the murder of Mexican citizens and for other illegal activities here in Mexico."

Anxious to complete the task at hand and tired of the conversation, Wheeler said, "We can sort this out later, can we not, Colonel?"

Nodding, Kosterlitzky replied briskly, "You and your men will follow us. When we arrive at the hacienda, you will split your Ranger Company in two — one group to attack the north flank, the other to attack the south flank. My men will also split into two forces and attack the front and rear of the hacienda. Is that clear?"

"Yes," said Wheeler impatiently.

The Rurales colonel wheeled his white horse and galloped south, followed by his men. The Rangers fell in behind. The sun appeared in the east, and the sight of it warmed a chilled Joaquin Campbell.

***

Kosterlitzky had sent several Rurales to take out all the sentries some time before the main group arrived at the hacienda. There were no explicit instructions on the treatment of prisoners or the attack itself. It was a bold, quick strike meant to overrun the bandits.

Joaquin touched his spurs to the paint's flanks as he rode hard to keep up with Wheeler and the others charging in from the north. They rode past several orchards and gardens straight toward the main house; a large, beautiful *hacienda* at the top of a small hill. Joaquin saw a cross atop one of the buildings; several other buildings had bell towers at their crest. As they neared the *hacienda*, they began taking fire. Miraculously, none of the Rangers' saddles were emptied.

Grasping his father's old .45 Colt in his right fist, he cocked it as the cold wind tore at his face. A bandit wearing a large sombrero appeared to his right holding a rifle, and as he brought the weapon up to his shoulder, Joaquin shot him in the chest. Men were screaming, yelling; shots zinged by as Joaquin leaned low next to his horse's neck. The paint horse took him through the *portada* or arched entrance into the *patio* or courtyard. The ivy covered walls led him first to the *cochiera* or coach house and then to the *cuardras* or horse stalls.

He saw Chapo Carter horseback near two large double doors. Carter leveled his double-barreled shotgun at the glass doors and fired. They shattered showering glass everywhere. Carter spurred his horse inside. Joaquin urged his reluctant horse to follow. A bullet narrowly missed him. Turning, he shot his assailant from the roof top. Then Joaquin and his horse were inside the hacienda.

Swiftly dismounting, he took cover behind a marble column in the large room, Carter behind another. Heavy fire came from within the hacienda. A mounted Rurale astride a frisky, black horse galloped in.

Joaquin saw in horror the man held a dynamite stick, the fuse lit. *What the ...oh, my God.*

The Mexican lawman made a difficult target as he leaned to the far right side of his horse. Suddenly, he lurched upright and threw the dynamite stick through one of the open windows. The dynamite exploded with a thunderous roar as the interior of the building exploded outward.

Joaquin ducked down behind the protective column as debris—wood, adobe and concrete—flew from the side of the house. The firing from inside the hacienda ceased. After reloading, Joaquin transferred his .45 Colt to his injured left hand, grasping it tightly. He drew the other pistol from his shoulder holster on the left side, and charged the house. Carter was next to him as he entered the smoke-filled room.

Stepping clear of the opening, Joaquin searched through the dense smoke for armed adversaries. Bloodied bodies were strewn across the wreckage in the large banquet room, but he saw no one alive or moving. He and Carter covered each other as they moved tactically toward a door leading deeper into the interior of the hacienda itself.

They heard loud voices coming from the adjacent room. Joaquin took a deep breath, then slammed his shoulder into the door, forcing it inward. With both revolvers cocked and out in front of him, he darted through the opening and to the right to avoid being caught in the entrance funnel. Carter followed closely behind him, angling to the left.

Two Rurales had a large Anglo man up against the wall, his hands held high. They whirled around, but seeing the Rangers, returned their attention to the man. One of them cocked his pistol and held it against the man's skull. The Rurale laughed. "*Adios, cabron.*"

"*Espere!*" Joaquin leaped forward, holstering his revolvers. There was something about the man ... his size? "Wait!" He implored again, this time in English.

The Rurale looked puzzled, but did not fire.

"*Por favor.* Let me talk to him."

The Rurale hesitated. "No." He grinned. "I theenk I keel heem."

Joaquin grabbed his arm. "Please. Wait. Allow me to talk to this man." The Rurale looked sharply at Joaquin's hand on his gun arm.

"Your *Coronel* would want me to ask this man some questions." Joaquin removed his hand. "Let me *talk* to him. Then you can kill him, uh?"

Joaquin's eyes squarely met the Mexican lawman's. Slowly, the Rurale lowered his gun arm, de-cocking his revolver. He said nothing, but holstered his gun.

The large Anglo man against the wall smiled. "That's more like it. I'll not be treated like a common criminal. I have my rights, you know. By God, I'm an American citizen."

Joaquin peered at the man. He was heavy-set, wearing an expensive suit and tie and his boots were polished. The man sported a large belly and a red face. He spoke with a loud, commanding voice. "Now, see here."

Joaquin hit him squarely between the eyes, knocking him back against the adobe wall. The man struggled to keep his balance, his eyes glazed. Joaquin said, "Well now, Mister Ben Hyde, in case you haven't noticed, this here ain't America." Reaching over, he pulled cigars from the inside pocket of the man's suit. He tossed one to each of the men standing near him. "You *are* Wade, aren't you?"

"What ... if I am?" the man stammered.

"As you ought to know, Hyde, this is *Mexico*, and you're *guilty* till proven innocent down here."

With difficulty, the fat man pulled at his suit coat. He was sweating profusely. "Look, there's no need for this. I have money—lots of it. I can pay you men well to allow me to slip away." Removing his suit jacket, he tossed it to the floor and began rolling up his sleeves. Perspiration rolled down his cheeks.

"You're charged with running guns across the border and worse—with the *murder* of several Rangers and countless other American citizens, *damn you!*" shouted Joaquin.

"*Prove it!* I only protect my legitimate business interests." He looked at Joaquin and Carter. "You men should understand I can't be held responsible for everything my employees may do." Hyde finished rolling up his sleeves.

"You're finished. If the Rurales don't 'dobe wall you, we'll take you back to hang, Hyde." Joaquin turned away in disgust. He heard Chapo Carter yell to him and swung around quickly. Hyde was drawing a small derringer from his vest pocket. Without thinking, Joaquin drew his .45 Colt and fired almost point-blank. He felt a small tug at the fabric of his jacket on the right side. He cocked the single-action revolver with his left thumb and fired again, and again.

Hit multiple times in the chest, Hyde gasped and slid to the floor. His head drooped forward.

"Thet's some shootin', kid," drawled Carter. "Elliott'd be proud of ya."

The two Rurales stood with their mouths open, unable to speak. The shooting had taken just seconds. Joaquin looked down at the dead man. He twirled his six-shooter on his right index finger as Elliott had shown him, forward then backward, allowing it to settle by its own weight into the holster at his side.

He started to turn away, then with a frown on his face, he swung back and peered down at Hyde slumped against the blood-smeared wall. Kneeling, he picked up Hyde's right arm. As he looked more closely, his heart began to pound intensely in his chest. On the dead man's forearm, a tattoo clearly displayed the same inscription he had seen written in blood at Ranger Bill Calhoun's murder scene.

CHAPTER THIRTY-THREE
February 17, 1909

Sitting at his desk at Ranger Headquarters in Naco, Arizona Territory, Captain Harry Wheeler finished reading Joaquin Campbell's report. The young Ranger had become one of his finest officers, and his recent actions and subsequent report substantiated it. Wheeler sighed deeply. Sadly, it would seem his Rangers were at the top of their game too late.

He flipped through the pages. Several members of Hyde's outlaw band were "coaxed" by Kosterlitzky and the Rurales to tell everything they knew of Hyde's involvement in various crimes in the United States and Mexico. The report detailed Hyde's personal culpability in the death of Ranger Calhoun. He had fired the fatal shot, ending the Ranger's life as he lay dying. Hyde's hired gun, Slydell Coburn, had murdered the prostitute that night. Coburn had beaten and hung the Chinaman Hao Li with the assistance of several of his thugs.

It was Hyde who had arrogantly ordered the attacks at the Cienega Ranch headquarters and Elliott's Ranch on the San Pedro River. Those attacks had cost him dearly in the loss of a large number of his men; subsequently, it had been easier for the Rangers and Rurales to take the outlaw compound in Mexico.

Wheeler pushed the report aside. He was mad— mad as hell! Then he was depressed. He stood, placed his hands in his pants pockets as he stared out the window.

Dammit! Everything's lost. Everything we've worked so hard for all these eight years. He had been waiting at the Capital two days prior, waiting impatiently for an opportunity to speak to the Territorial Legislature on behalf of his beloved Arizona Rangers. The damned politicians wouldn't even allow him the courtesy to speak. He had always disliked politicians; he found most self-serving and inept. And now he had a great distaste of any of them, a gut-wrenching hatred for all of them regardless of party lines.

Governor Joseph Kibbey, a Republican, had become a target of the democratically controlled legislature for several years. Outnumbering the Republicans ten to two in the Council, and eighteen to six in the House of Representatives, the Democrats finally had their chance for revenge at the Governor in submitting and subsequently passing a bill to repeal the Ranger Act of 1901 and abolish the Ranger company, once and for all.

The Governor, several sheriffs, and former Arizona Ranger Captain Burt Mossman appealed to the legislature to no avail. As of February 15, 1909, the Rangers had ceased to exist. And to further complicate matters, there was no transitional period. Wheeler had men out in the field with no way to contact them immediately. What was to come of the numerous pending criminal cases, men arrested by the Rangers and jailed or those out on bail awaiting trial? Wheeler cursed under his breath. All the sacrifices, the hard work, the deaths—in the line of duty of Tafolla, Calhoun, and Kidder?

Wheeler sat down at his desk. Understaffed, there were nineteen men on the payroll when the Rangers were abolished. He had contacted most of these by various means over the past two days, but several remained out there with no knowledge their law enforcement commissions were no longer valid. Jack Redman was chasing rustlers in the Chiracahua Mountains and Joaquin Campbell was on leave at home.

Standing, Wheeler placed his flat-brimmed, gray Stetson hat on his head and squared his shoulders. Sending a rider out to find Redman, he decided to ride out to tell young Campbell personally, then take the extra time to swing by Elliott' place.

The ex-Ranger Captain slipped on his wool jacket buttoned it up as he gazed at the five-pointed, silver star lying on his desk. It was inscribed, "Captain, Arizona Rangers." Shaking his head with a deep frown on his dark face, he strode past the badge resting on the desk to the door. Yes, he owed them that ... and much more.

CHAPTER THIRTY-FOUR
February 20, 1909

Joaquin Campbell finished the morning chores, milking, feeding the horses and dogie calves in the barn. He stood in front of the barn as he had done numerous times in his life. The winter air was crisp with a slight breeze out of the northwest. As he stood motionless, the sunrise magically appeared over the Whetstone Mountains to the east, lighting up an orange sky filled with white clouds of several designs. *God, I truly love Arizona.*

Feeling the chill, he pulled the collar of his wool coat up around his neck. He had been home for about a week on leave, and it meant everything to him. Spending valuable time with his family was something he'd needed badly. Captain Wheeler ordered him to take the time off, and he was very appreciative of the gesture. His thoughts were interrupted by someone tugging at his leg. He knelt down and hugged the old shaggy dog.

"*Solo Vino*," He stroked and patted the stock dog standing next to him. The old dog's eyes closed, his mouth opened with his tongue protruding as he savored the attention. Standing, Joaquin said, "Come on, boy! I'll race you for the house."

Running hard, the young Ranger was easily outdistanced by his four-legged friend. As he reached the porch, the dog was waiting for him near the front door to the casita he and Carmen called their home. "I'm going to stop calling you *viejo, Sol.* You run faster than ever, boy."

Leaving the dog on the porch, he burst into the house. "Carmen!"

His wife turned from the wood cook stove; she held tortillas in her hands. "You don't have to yell, *mi querido*, I'm right here." Her long black hair cascaded along her shoulders. Placing the tortillas next to the stove, she brushed hair back from her face. Joaquin knew she preferred to arrange her hair into two braids. However, last night she had removed the braids just for him. He walked to her and hugged her tightly and kissed her. She smiled brightly at him, and he could see those pretty, brown eyes were dancing—no sadness.

Carmen placed her arms around his shoulders and returned his kiss. He pulled her closely to him, kissing the nape of her neck. He smelled smoke. *The tortillas!*

Carmen gently pushed him away, as she grabbed the burnt tortillas. "*Joaquin*. I'm trying to cook breakfast."

He laughed. "Where's my buddy?" he asked.

"He's still in bed, sleeping."

"Elliott'd be on him like flies on *caca* for sleeping in this late."

They were both silent for a few minutes, then she said, "I really wish you wouldn't use that kind of talk, Joaquin."

"Okay." He walked into the small bedroom, and looked down at his son. The boy was awake, lying under the warm blankets on the bed.

"Hi, Daddy."

Joaquin sat down on the edge of the bed. "Hi yourself, *mijo*."

The small boy reached out and touched his father's hand. "I'm glad you're home, Daddy."

"Me, too." Joaquin hugged his son.

Carmen called out to him from the kitchen. "Someone's riding in, Joaquin." Her voice showed concern.

He rose and walked to the front window. Reaching for the .45 Colt in the belt holster hanging on a peg by the door, he peered more intently at the lone horseman riding toward the *casita*. Grinning, he left the gun in the holster. "No worries, Carmen. It's Cap'n Wheeler." He looked at his wife as he opened the door latch and stepped out onto the porch. He did not fail to notice the worried look was still on her face.

***

Carmen poured hot black coffee for Harry Wheeler as he sat at the kitchen table. "Like I was saying, Joaquin, the Rangers are finished—they abolished us when they repealed the Ranger Act several days ago."

Joaquin shook his head in disbelief and he took a sip of hot coffee. "You told us they would, Cap'n, but I just couldn't believe it."

"Believe it, son. We're out of a job."

As Carmen tended to the cook stove, she couldn't concentrate on what she was doing. *Oh, thank you, God! Joaquin can stay here with us now.* The Rangers were abolished! It was the best news she had heard in a long, long time.

"Captain, would you like more pancakes?" Her voice was unable to hide her elation at the news.

Wheeler smiled at her. "No thank you, ma'am. I'm full, and I need to get along over to Elliott's place. I want to talk with Megan ... offer any help she might accept."

He stood up from the table. "Thanks again for breakfast. I'd best be moving on." He turned to Joaquin. "I might run for sheriff of Cochise County one of these days. I'd like to have you for a deputy, son."

Carmen's heart almost stopped. She could scarcely breathe.

Standing, Joaquin reached out and shook the Ranger Captain's hand. "Well, sir. I take that as a high compliment. It would be an honor to serve under you again, but I reckon I got lots to do here, and I'm enjoying my family."

Wheeler was persistent. "Don't decide today, Joaquin. Take your time."

Joaquin followed him to the door and out onto the porch. Wheeler mounted his black gelding. He looked down at the young Ranger. "You take care, Joaquin. I appreciate your dedicated service to the territory and to me. You've become one of my finest Rangers."

"Thank you, sir. Good luck to you."

Carmen walked to where Joaquin stood on the porch watching his old boss riding away. She took his hand, and together they watched silently as the horseman disappeared from sight.

Joaquin said, "Well, here I am lollygagging when there's so much work to be done."

Carmen pulled him close to her. A smile worked at the corner of her mouth. "Wel-l-l now, how about lollygagging with me, *mister?*"

With a tremor in his voice, Joaquin said, "I reckon the work could wait ...?"

CHAPTER THIRTY-FIVE

Megan dabbed at the dirty skillet in the wash basin with a wash cloth. It did not come clean. As she grew more frustrated, tears ran down her cheeks. *Oh God, I can't live without him. I don't want to live anymore!* She slumped over the wash basin, her hands immersed in the hot water doing nothing. Sobs racked her body as the skillet slipped from her hands, splashing soapy water into her face already wet from tears. Then she cried outright; the agony and deep-seated pain kept too long inside her escaped with a strangled half-scream. Her body shook with spasms as tears streamed in torrents.

Stumbling out the door onto the porch, she sat on the steps. She bent over, her hands on her knees. Grasping her head in both hands, she cried out loud to her God, "*Why?* Why did you take my husband?" Silence. There was only silence and the darkness of the night. She sobbed again in agony.

"Mother?" a soft voice said from behind her.

Megan's head came up. She sighed deeply and shuddered uncontrollably.

Tim Campbell crawled up behind her and touched her shaking shoulders. His voice was soft but firm. "Are you okay, Mom?"

She sighed heavily again, patted his hand on her shoulder. "I ... I'm not ... doing well, Timmy."

The young boy slid around and sat next to her on the porch. He placed his arm around her shoulders, but said nothing. Megan cried again, tears pouring down her cheeks. She sobbed and shuddered, then coughed several times.

"It's *okay*, Mom. You need to cry it all out."

Megan reached over and grasped her son's hand for support. "What will I ... we do?"

"We'll go on living." The boy's calmness began to affect her; the shaking subsided. Several moments passed. He continued, "We can't give this place up now, Mom. It's become our home—for all of us, Li and Elliott, too."

She sobbed at the mention of his name then she took a deep breath. "Yes, Timmy. You're right."

"Joaquin and Carmen will help us with the spring roundup, and we must help them as well."

"*Yes.*" Thoughts ran through her head. "And my friend Sally said they were looking for a teacher at the school in St. David."

Tim pulled his mother to him. "Maybe they would hire me to work in the store there as well? I'll be fourteen soon. Elliott hired out to work the cattle drives when he was just fifteen."

Megan wiped at her face. They could make a go of it. Yes, they would do just that. She turned to Tim and smiled at him in the darkness. "Thank you, Tim. You're right, of course."

"I love you, Mom."

They hugged again, both needing the reassurance. "I love you, Timmy."

An owl hooted in the distance. As they sat quietly on the porch, each into their own thoughts, several mule deer passed by the ranch house unnoticed. Tim stirred and said softly to his mother, "You can pray with me, Mom. Elliott gave me his rosary and taught me the prayers."

He reached in his pocket and withdrew the old

brown rosary that Father Quinones had given Elliott so many years ago. "See?"

Megan reached over and touched his hands, then the rosary. She said nothing for several minutes. "Will you teach me how, son?"

***

Somehow, Tim remembered the prayers. Well, maybe he didn't get the words exactly right, but he figured the old Ranger most likely didn't get it perfect either. As he prayed with his mother, he knew in his heart it was the thought that counted, not mere words.

Somewhere way above them the stars twinkled in the southwestern sky, spurs clinked and a chuckle resounded in the night. "Wel-l-l now, thet boy has done some growin', ain't he? An' Megan ... ain't she the purtiest gal plumb west o' the Mississippi River?"

The owl hooted again. As the old Ranger looked down on his beloved family, he drawled, "I reckon I'll be see'n you again."

THE END

Other Books by John McLaughlin

Our Time in the Sun

This historically accurate account of an Old West group of lawmen, the Arizona Rangers, is an action-filled story complete with conflict, revenge, love, racism, and redemption in the Arizona Territory of 1903-04. Against the magnificent backdrop of the Southwest, the Rangers chase rustlers, help quell a major riot with miners in Morenci, and track the nefarious bandit, Indio Chacon, and his band of outlaws deep into the Sierra Madres in Mexico.

Elliott, a seasoned Ranger, struggles with his dark and violent past as he leads a contingent of Arizona Rangers stationed near the Mexican border. Along the way, Elliott finds time to mentor a young Ranger, Joaquin Campbell, who is short on law enforcement experience and life itself. Racism rears its ugly head as Campbell falls in love with a young Mexican woman.

This western adventure is the prequel to Red Sky at Morning.

"The man swallowed hard, placed his hands on his knees to catch a deep breath. He looked up at Elliott. 'I'm tellin' you to run, you damn fool! Bad men—kilt the bartender—stealin' money.' He licked his lips. 'I'm goin' ... to find ... ' Then he saw the silver stars on both men's shirts. 'Wait a minute—you are the law!'

Elliott dismissed the man, his eyes hard. 'Yessir ... thet's what we're here for.' He spoke to Joaquin without turning as he moved toward the door. 'When we go through the door—do it quick an' step to my left away from me.' With that he was gone, inside the saloon."

Purchase *Our Time in the Sun* on the web
www.johnmclaughlinbooks.com
Or visit with the author at
johnmclaughlinbooks@hotmail.com